THIS BOOK BELONGS TO

_____

KENDRA KANDLESTAR
AND THE CRACK IN KAZAH

KENDRA KANDLESTAR

AND THE CRACK IN KAZAH

BOOK
4

Written and Illustrated by
Lee Edward Födi

SIMPLY READ BOOKS

Published in 2014 by Simply Read Books
www.simplyreadbooks.com
Text & Illustrations © 2014 Lee Edward Födi

First published in 2011 by Brown Books Publishing Group

Library and Archives Canada Cataloguing in Publication

Födi, Lee Edward
Kendra Kandlestar and the Crack in Kazah / written and
illustrated by Lee Edward Födi.

ISBN 978-1-927018-28-6 (pbk.)

I. Title.

PS8611.O45K453 2014   jC813'.6   C2013-906054-5

We gratefully acknowledge for their financial support of our publishing
program the Canada Council for the Arts, the BC Arts Council, and the
Government of Canada through the Canada Book Fund (CBF).

Manufactured in Canada.

Book design by Lee Edward Födi
Cover design by Sara Gillingham

10 9 8 7 6 5 4 3 2 1

To
Mom and Dad,
because you
too were once
young.

LIST OF CHAPTERS

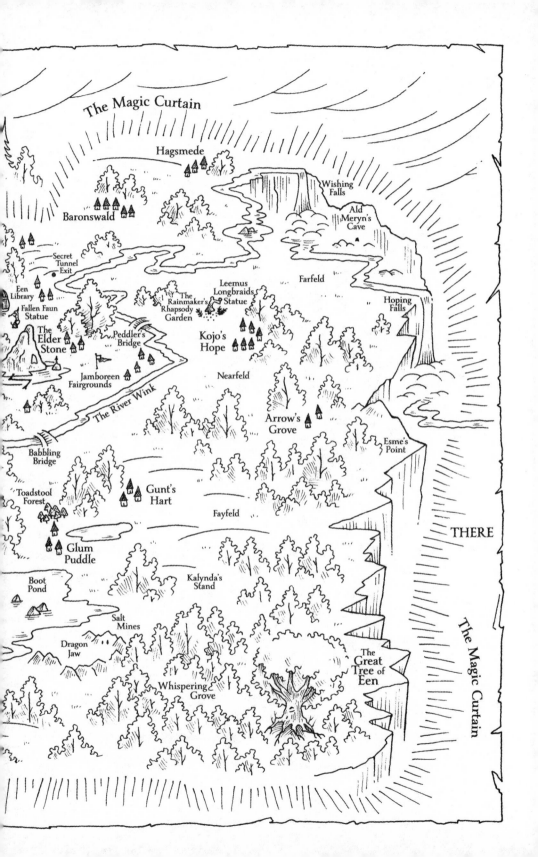

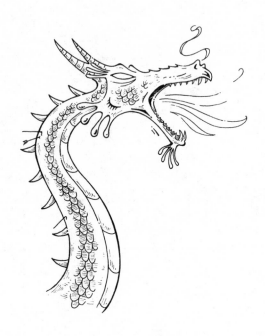

CHAPTER 1

How Kendra Heard the Danger

As this tale unfolds and your mind leaves the humdrum drone of everyday life, you will find yourself wandering along a familiar path, where mysterious characters lurk around each bend, where certain danger lingers in every shadow. Indeed, you know this path well—for this is the road to adventure, and you, my young dreamer, have traveled it before.

Perhaps you have found yourself hiding behind the long beard of an ancient wizard as he weaves his magic against the fire of a ferocious dragon. Or perhaps you have crept behind the tattered cape of a brave explorer, through the bone-biting shadows of a dark dungeon, seeking escape from monstrous fiends. Perhaps you have even found yourself amidst the roar and rumble of a mighty battle, dodging claws and talons, fists and feet.

1

If your imagination has taken you to such places, then you know that no adventure happens without a long journey. We do not find ourselves thrust immediately before the dragon, or suddenly lost in the dungeon maze, or so quickly catapulted into the roar of battle. Indeed, we must begin with that first step upon adventure's path. We must trek through places strange and unknown. The journey, as you know, is sometimes as important as the final destination.

Ah! Such has always been the case with our young heroine, Kendra Kandlestar. If you are familiar at all with her adventures, then you know she comes from the quiet Land of Een, tucked between the cracks of Here and There. The Eens, of course, are an ancient race—some say older than even elves or dwarves. The Eens are a small people and are known for many things: their long braids, their ability to speak to animals, and—perhaps most of all—for their shy and timid nature. Indeed, they prefer to stay hidden behind the magic curtain that protects them from the outside world. But Kendra has never been an ordinary Een. We have seen her cross rivers and wastelands, descend into mines and dungeons, and climb cliffs and castle towers. And now she will undertake her most difficult journey yet. Perhaps you will be surprised to know that she will end just as she has begun, for in this tale Kendra will not visit new lands. She will find herself only in those places she has been before.

Then how can this be a journey, you ask? Ah—there lies the key to this tale. Imagine, if you will, not a journey to where—but a journey to *when*.

So, now, questions are swirling through your mind, just like the flakes of snow on the cold and bleak morning when our story begins. Here, amidst a symphony of winter wind, a magical airship chugs across the sky. It looks like a giant bird, with sails for wings and windows for eyes. The ship is called the *Big Bang*, and amongst its crew is a wizard's apprentice: twelve-year-old Kendra Kandlestar.

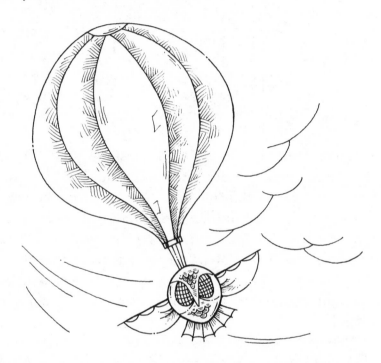

On this winter's morn, Kendra was sitting in a dark chamber below deck, her mind ablaze with questions as she pondered the mysteries of Een magic. She did not enjoy sitting in quiet meditation. Even with her eyes closed and her hands outstretched, it was a grueling task to focus on the moment, to think only of the present.

Instead, Kendra thought of the past. She thought of the future. She thought of her brother Kiro, and all that he had done, all that he was meant to do. And yet Kiro, in a way, was

no more. Long ago, he had been transformed into Trooogul the Unger, a beastly creature with tusks and claws and crooked limbs, and it was difficult to know whose side he was on. Trooogul had stolen the dark stone known as the Shard from Greeve, a fragment of an ancient warlock's cauldron. As far as Kendra knew, Trooogul was intent on rebuilding that vile cauldron—which meant resurrecting a curse that could transform the entire Een race into monsters, just like Trooogul himself.

He's somewhere out there, in the lands below, headed towards the City on the Storm, Kendra told herself. *We must find him before it's too late.*

"Humph."

Kendra opened her eyes and gazed upon her master. He sat across from her, mirroring her pose, and as still as a statue. He was ancient and frail, with a beard so long and white that some Eens claimed he used it to sweep his floors. But Kendra knew better, for not only was the wizard her master, but her uncle as well. With her family having long ago disappeared, ornery old Uncle Griffinskitch had raised her from the time

she was a baby. He never swept his floors, with his beard or otherwise. Sweeping was *her* job.

Uncle Griffinskitch looked older than ever. His face was a crisscross of cracks, as if someone had taken a putty knife to clay, and his beard was as white as the surrounding mountain tops. He even wore spectacles now—an old hand-me-down pair from Professor Bumblebean. Of course, at this moment, Uncle Griffinskitch didn't need his spectacles. Even though his eyes were closed, Kendra felt as if the old man was glaring right into her soul.

"You must focus, child," Uncle Griffinskitch admonished. "If you wish to master Een magic, then you must quiet your mind, tune yourself to your wand."

Kendra's eyes turned to the small stick of wood that lay in front of her. She had received her wand months ago, but she still had trouble understanding its power. Kendra looked back at her uncle. His own wand was more like a staff, twisted and gnarled, its length a symbol of his mastery of Een magic. The wand stood beside him, without support, as if it had a mind and will of its own.

"Remember, the wands do not give us magic," Uncle Griffinskitch instructed, his eyes remaining shut.

"Then why have them at all?" Kendra asked.

"A wand is like a musical instrument," the old man replied.

"Like the narfoo?" Kendra asked, thinking of the golden horn-shaped instrument that hung on their wall back at home. The narfoo seemed to have a hundred valves and keys—far too complicated for Kendra to imagine playing. Come to think of it, she had never seen Uncle Griffinskitch play it either.

"Yes, the narfoo, if you wish," Uncle Griffinskitch grunted impatiently. "If you want to make music, then you need the narfoo. But the instrument itself does not make beautiful sounds; it only amplifies that which the player finds within."

Kendra sighed, and tugged nervously at one of the seven braids that protruded from her head of brown hair. "Was it this difficult to train my mother?"

Uncle Griffinskitch's eyes fluttered open. "Where does this question come from?"

Kendra fiddled with her hair, not sure what to say.

"She asked as many questions as you, that is for certain," the old wizard offered. "She had a strong will—and more attitude than a giant with a sliver in his toe."

Kendra had seen a giant or two in her time; she couldn't help thinking that, for a giant, the nearest thing to a sliver would be a small tree.

"Your mind wanders again," Uncle Griffinskitch accused.

"Sorry," Kendra said. "You didn't really like her, did you? My mother, I mean."

A soft growl escaped from the wizard's lips. Kendra knew it was difficult for him to talk about such matters. After all, Kendra's mother was his own sister. She was just as long-lost to him as she was to Kendra. "Your mother and I did not often see eye to eye," Uncle Griffinskitch admitted. "But my love for her was as deep as my beard is long."

"Is," Kendra said. "You mean *is*. She's still alive."

"Humph," Uncle Griffinskitch muttered. It was the type of humph that meant the discussion was over. "We shall return to our meditation, this time with our wands."

Kendra nodded, lifted her wand, and closed her eyes again. She took a deep breath.

Focus, came her uncle's voice—but he wasn't speaking out loud. The words just popped into Kendra's mind. He was speaking to her through their wands. *Feel the world around us,* he said.

Yes, master.

What can you see?

My eyes are closed!

See without your eyes, Uncle Griffinskitch told her. *Deeper breaths. Let your mind expand. The world surrounds us, alive and vibrant. Tell me what you see.*

Kendra wrinkled her nose, wishing she could tug at one of her braids. But instead she followed her uncle's command by taking another deep breath, trying to focus. For several minutes she just sat there, quietly breathing as the sound of her uncle's voice whispered inside her. Slowly, Kendra felt her mind begin to drift, as if she was entering a dream.

Now tell me, came her uncle's voice, *what can you see?*

A picture began to appear in Kendra's mind, hazy and white. *Clouds,* Kendra told her uncle. *An endless stretch of clouds.* Then she saw something sharp and black amidst the white. *There are rocky crags ahead,* Kendra added. *We should warn Ratchet, so he doesn't crash the ship.*

The ship will be fine, her uncle said. *Stay with the moment. What can you taste?*

Water, Kendra replied. *It's cold . . . wait, not water; snow. I can feel it melting on my tongue! It's snowing outside.*

Good. Now, what do you smell?

Smoke on the wind. Someone has lit a fire, far below, on the ground. Kendra now felt light as air, as if she was no longer in her body, no longer on the ship. The sensation was incredible.

Keep it going, Uncle Griffinskitch urged. *Tell me, what do you hear?*

Kendra tuned her mind. *I hear someone telling a story. It's the legend of how two Eengels with braided hair appeared before the first elders of Een. I think we must be close to home! But still, how can I hear that from way up here?*

Distance, size—even time, these are but barriers in our minds. We must train ourselves to climb these walls! Our frail minds may fret over such obstacles, but the magic of Een does not. Yes, the magic. Tune to it, Kendra. It can take you anywhere, if you so allow. Now, keep seeking, Kendra. What else do you hear?

Kendra breathed and let her senses wander. *Snow is falling on the trees, on the mountains. There's a murmur in the wind. There's a—*

Suddenly, a dreadful shriek pierced her mind, like an arrow splitting a melon. She dropped her wand with a clatter and clutched her ears—and the sound was instantly gone. Her eyes flew open, only to see Uncle Griffinskitch staring back at her, his wrinkled face gaping in surprise. He had heard it too.

"Uncle—,"

But the old wizard was already rising to his feet in a flourish of white beard. "Quickly, Kendra," he beckoned. "To the ship's deck. We're under attack!"

CHAPTER 2

The
Battle
in the
Clouds

Have you ever been bolted awake by an alarm or siren? Then you might know exactly how Kendra felt as she scrambled to her feet and followed her uncle to the ship's deck. One second she had been sitting in a peaceful trance— and the next forced to spring into action. It was like wading knee-deep in mud and suddenly being asked to sprint.

Yet, when they reached the deck, the skies were calm and serene, and the rest of the crew seemed not the least bit alarmed. Here was Ratchet Ringtail, the large grey raccoon, piloting the ship and whistling a quiet tune. Here was Professor Bumblebean, the tall and gangly Een, muffled in a scarf and mittens as he cheerfully paced back and forth, studying one of his hefty books. Here was Jinx, the tiny grasshopper with the mountain of strength, sharpening her

9

sword. And here too, was Kendra's best friend, Oki the mouse, sweeping the snow that was beginning to pile up in little drifts upon the deck. It was the perfect picture of tranquility.

"I don't get it," Kendra said. "I thought—,"

Uncle Griffinskitch didn't let her finish. "Captain Ringtail!" he boomed. "Turn the ship about at once! We're about to be attacked."

"Eek!" Oki squealed, running over to hide behind Kendra's cloak. "By what?"

"I do say," Professor Bumblebean declared, peering over his glasses. "It seems a perfectly quiet morn, not a speck in the—,"

Then the shriek came again, the same one Kendra had heard in her trance. Everyone rushed to the ship's railing and peered into the clouds. Kendra could feel Oki pressing nervously against her legs.

"Don't think of eggs!" he fretted. "Don't think of eggs!'

"Eggs?" Kendra asked.

"You know me," he said timidly. "I always try *not* to think of something when we're in danger. It helps me forget I'm scared. Ratchet suggested that I try eggs."

As far as Kendra was concerned, Oki's technique never seemed to work. Tugging braids worked best for her, which is exactly what she did as she returned her gaze to the sky.

"I still don't see anything," Jinx murmured, her antennae twitching.

Then a squiggly black line appeared against the sky. It was soon followed by another, then another, until there were a dozen of the twisting shapes—each of them shrieking as loudly as the next and causing a monstrous cacophony.

"Skarm!" Jinx exclaimed. "A whole swarm of them!"

"Well, if we are to be precise," Professor Bumblebean corrected, "in a group, skarm are normally referred to as a 'senate.' So what we have, my dear Jinx, is—,"

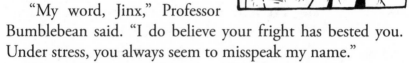

"Oh stuff it, *Bumblenerd*," Jinx retorted. "This is no time for a lecture!"

"My word, Jinx," Professor Bumblebean said. "I do believe your fright has bested you. Under stress, you always seem to misspeak my name."

"Listen here, *Dumblebean* . . ."

Their banter continued, but Kendra ignored it, focusing instead on the terrifying sight of the approaching skarm. They were dreadful creatures, with long worm-like bodies and reptilian tongues that zipped in and out like whips. Each skarm had a pair of feathered wings, but—and this was their most alarming feature—only a single giant eye that blinked and twitched above a row of crooked fangs.

"I do say," Professor Bumblebean declared, turning his attention away from Jinx. "This whole vessel is supported by one enormous balloon. If those skarm manage to puncture it with claw or tooth, we shall direly crash!"

"No one's going to get diarrhea and crash," Ratchet said. "I'm the best air pilot in Een."

"Uh, Ratchet?" Oki said. "You're the *only* air pilot in Een. And Professor Bumblebean didn't say 'diarrhea,' he said—,"

"Humph!" Uncle Griffinskitch interrupted—it was the type of humph that meant he had heard enough chatter. "We'll have to fight," the old wizard declared. "Jinx, prepare your weapons. Ratchet, does this ship have any defenses?"

"Of course!" Ratchet replied, seeming almost offended by the question. "The *Big Bang* comes armed with six power-ful cannons."

"What do they fire?" the wizard asked.

"A little something I call *Snot Shot*," Ratchet replied with a ring of pride in his voice.

Kendra groaned. Ratchet considered himself an amateur wizard and an inventor of extraordinary talent. Most of his inventions were "extraordinarily absurd" (in Uncle Griffin-skitch's words), but Kendra knew that Ratchet was capable of coming up with an ingenious idea every now and then—espe-cially since he had taken Oki as his apprentice. The *Big Bang* was certainly a marvelous invention. *Snot Shot*, on the other hand, was something Kendra wasn't so sure about.

"Er . . . Ratchet?" Kendra asked. "Please tell me *Snot Shot* isn't what I think it is? You're not going to be firing dragon mucus or some other nonsense, are you?"

"Of course not!" Ratchet said. "Yeesh!"

"It's just a powder, Kendra," Oki explained. "But if you get hit with it, your nose will start to itch and twitch—and then you start to gush . . . well, you know. Snot."

"You bone-headed, burp-brained buffoons," Jinx scolded. "How do think your stupid cannons are going to help? Do skarm even have noses?"

"We're about to find out!" Ratchet declared, but now Ken-dra could barely hear him over the shrill of the approaching skarm.

Uncle Griffinskitch quickly organized everyone into position. Professor Bumblebean assumed command of the helm while Ratchet scrambled along the deck, clicking switches and springing hatches to reveal two rows of cannons on either side of the ship. Oki rushed behind, stuffing the barrels with tiny balls of crystallized powder (the *Snot Shot*, Kendra assumed). Jinx leapt to the railing, one claw clutching a rope for support, the other three brandishing weapons. As for Kendra and Uncle Griffinskitch, they readied their wands.

Aim for the eyes, came Uncle Griffinskitch's voice inside Kendra's mind. *A simple zap—that's all it will take to repel them. Remember: focus!*

He made it sound so easy. Kendra allowed herself one last tug of her braids—and then the onslaught began.

If you have ever seen a flock of crows discover a scrap of food upon the road, then you know how they caw and claw—even at each other—as they shred their carrion to bits. It can be a beastly scene; but now imagine that the crows are skarm and the scrap of dinner the cloud ship, and you will get an idea of the deadly battle that erupted around Kendra.

There were so many skarm that their long wings blotted out the sun; everywhere Kendra looked there was a tongue, a claw, or an enormous, bulbous eye. The whole ship quaked and shuddered—at first Kendra thought it was just from the howls of the skarm, but then she realized that the monstrous worms were ramming the sides. The *Big Bang* bobbed and swayed like a leaf in a whirlpool.

Kendra clutched the railing of the ship, panicking. How could she focus amidst the chaotic roar of battle?

Try! came her uncle's voice.

She looked up and saw the old wizard in action, a whirl of white as he spun and sprang about the deck, sending out crackles of lightning from his gnarled wand. Kendra watched, spellbound, as one of the wizard's zaps glanced off the wing of

the nearest skarm; it retreated slightly, then prepared to attack again—only to be struck right in the face by a sudden burst of *Snot Shot!*

The skarm sputtered and coughed; for a moment it looked like nothing would happen, then suddenly it began to ooze green. It was a revolting sight, but one that filled Kendra with relief, for the skarm was soon so overcome with its own slime that it dropped out of view.

"One down!" Ratchet cheered in triumph.

It seemed to make no difference; another skarm quickly took its place and soared straight towards Kendra with its deadly claws extended.

"Don't just stand there!" Jinx growled as she thrust a spear over Kendra's head and right into the skarm's open mouth. The immense worm howled in pain and veered away.

Kendra gave her head a shake and raised her wand of Eenwood. With the next skarm upon her, she found the words in her head:

Crackle of light
Join the fight!
Banish and blight
With all my might!

Her wand blazed with energy, but struck the skarm with little more than a spark—all it seemed to do was anger the great wriggler. With a roar it thumped the deck with its massive tail; the ship rocked wildly, and Kendra watched in horror as Jinx lost her footing and slipped over the side.

"JINX!" Kendra charged towards the railing where her friend had disappeared, but she never made it; a long skarm tongue zipped out and hit her squarely in the chest. She was sent sprawling across the deck and plowed right into little Oki. They ended up in a tangled heap—but not for long. Kendra felt something wrap around her leg and yank her free. She looked back and, to her horror, saw a skarm tongue twisted around her like a vine. The menacing worm lifted her into the air, towards its giant, gaping maw.

Even over all the tumultuous noise, Kendra could hear Oki eeking from below. It helped her gather her wits—lifting her wand, she sent a bolt of lightning at the skarm and walloped it right in the eye. It dropped her immediately, and now Kendra was plummeting through the sky. With her wand in her right hand, she desperately reached out with her left and caught hold of a broken suspension rope that was swinging from the *Big Bang*. She stopped with such a jerk that she lost hold of her wand; it spiraled away, through the sky below her.

"Days of Een!" she cried. "Uncle Griffinskitch is going to kill me."

At least now she had two hands to cling to the rope. There she hung, twisting and turning in midair like bait on a hook beneath the shadow of the *Big Bang*, which lurched and listed in the ongoing attack.

It didn't take long for one of the skarm to find her. As the rope twisted around, Kendra found herself staring right into the bulging eye of the biggest skarm she had seen yet. Drool gushed from its mouth like a waterfall.

Then something else caught Kendra's attention and she let out a gasp of horror—for that something terrified her even more than the skarm. It was the worm's rider. There, straddled upon the back of the skarm like some sort of knight upon a demented steed, was none other than one of Kendra's greatest enemies: Agent Lurk.

CHAPTER 3

The Rider on the Skarm

There's nothing worse than running into your most miserable enemy when you're already in a spot of trouble. It's like being kept after school, only to find yourself sitting next to the class bully. Agent Lurk was worse than a class bully. He was one of the most vile and insidious Eens that Kendra had ever known, and now she was dangling right in front of him.

The last time Kendra had seen Agent Lurk was in the Rumble Pit, amidst the clash of deadly gladiators. She had been half-convinced that he had met his end there, beneath the swat of a Krake's tail, but here he was, yet again, and looking as ominous as ever. He wore a long cloak that concealed every part of his body except for his two talon-like hands, which were grayish and misshapen; on one finger he wore a large and brooding purple ring. As for the cloak, Kendra knew its power. At any moment Agent Lurk could turn invisible.

For the present, Kendra could see him, and it made her desperately wish that she had a free hand so that she could tug a braid. Like a shadow, Agent Lurk had chased her across sea and forest—and now sky. She had no idea how he had tracked her down, but there was no doubt what he wanted from her: the Shard from Greeve, that stone of dark and destructive magic.

Doesn't he know Trooogul has it? she wondered.

There was no time to dwell on the matter, for Agent Lurk now pulled his skarm alongside Kendra and with one cruel claw snatched her aboard his slimy mount. There was no saddle on the skarm, and immediately Kendra felt herself begin to slip from the beast's back. She threw herself against the skarm's worm-like skin, clenching with both hands and feet. It was disgusting.

As for Agent Lurk, he seemed completely at ease on the skarm's back. He loomed over Kendra and hissed, "The Shard! Give it to me, girl!"

Kendra strained her neck and glared up at him. "I don't—,"

Then, suddenly, Jinx was there. She seemed to appear from thin air, leaping aboard the skarm and striking Lurk right in the chest with one of her long legs. The tiny grasshopper soon had the nasty agent pinned against one of the skarm's wings.

"Well, if it isn't *Agent Twerp*!" Jinx said.

Kendra blinked—hadn't she seen Jinx plunge to certain death only moments ago? "H-h-how . . . ," Kendra stammered.

"I have wings, you know," Jinx retorted, not daring to take her eyes from Lurk. "I fluttered down and landed right on

18

top of one of these slimy worms. I've been playing hop-skarm ever since—until I landed here. Oh, by the way, I think you dropped this." The grasshopper tossed Kendra her wand.

"How did you find it?" Kendra asked with a sigh of relief.

"It landed right on my head when I was hopping skarm," Jinx explained. "Lucky for you I managed to catch it before it bounced away."

"A touching tale," Agent Lurk quipped. "Now you can release me, bug."

"Sure," Jinx said, sneering into Lurk's shadowy hood. "Just as soon as you get us off this slimy slug."

Agent Lurk's only response was to turn invisible, and it suddenly looked as if Jinx had one leg standing on empty air. "Don't worry," Jinx told Kendra. "I can't see him, but I can feel him beneath my foot. He's still here."

Then Kendra heard Lurk give a sharp hoot, and the skarm, upon hearing this command from its master, began circling upwards in a dizzying spiral until they were higher than the *Big Bang*.

"Hang on!" Kendra cried.

"Don't worry, I've got this little creep!" Jinx hollered.

"I meant hang onto the skarm—not Lurk!" Kendra called, closing her eyes and clenching even more tightly to the giant worm. Then she heard one of the ship's cannons fire, and in the next instant the skarm lurched beneath her. Kendra opened her eyes and saw that the flying wriggler had been struck full force by a ball of *Snot Shot*. At once the skarm began to ooze mucus—then it sneezed, so violently that Kendra, Jinx, and Lurk were all jostled from its back.

How many times am I going to fall today? Kendra wondered as she spun through the air.

But the *Big Bang* was beneath them now, and by some magic force they were all plucked from the sky and brought to a safe landing on the ship's deck.

"Are you all right?" Oki squealed, scampering over with the rest of the crew.

Kendra nodded. "What happened?" she murmured.

Uncle Griffinskitch tapped the deck with his staff. "Eenwood can do more than zap skarm," he grunted.

"A little help here, someone?" Jinx called.

Kendra turned to see the grasshopper struggling with Agent Lurk. The nasty Een had turned visible again, but only for a moment. He started to shimmer away.

Oki scampered over and threw a few flakes of powder into the empty space near Jinx's claw. "I think that's where his face is," Oki said.

"What are you doing?" Jinx demanded. "I don't want him spraying snot all over me."

"Oh, that wasn't *Snot Shot*—it's *Snore Galore*," Oki said, and indeed, they suddenly heard a loud snore and Lurk turned visible once again.

"My word!" Professor Bumblebean remarked. "I suppose that Agent Lurk's cloak doesn't function while he slumbers. How long until he arouses from his stupor?"

"I only gave him a few flakes," Oki replied. "He could wake at any moment!"

"Let us find a spot below deck for him," Uncle Griffinskitch advised. "I have a few questions to ask him once he awakens."

It was only then that Kendra noticed how quiet it was. "What happened to the skarm?"

"The cannons finally got the better of those slimy suckers," Ratchet declared proudly. "They've all retreated."

"Humph," Uncle Griffinskitch muttered.

"Well, your uncle's magic helped too," Ratchet added sheepishly.

"Come on," Jinx said. "We best get Lurky here tied up."

With her mighty strength, the small grasshopper hoisted Agent Lurk above her head, and they all followed as she carried him below deck to an empty storage compartment. Here Jinx bound Lurk with a length of rope and leaned him against the wall. For a moment they all just stood there, staring at him. Then Uncle Griffinskitch reached out and removed the large purple ring from Lurk's finger.

"There's something mysterious about that ring," Kendra said. "And it's cracked!"

"Aye," Uncle Griffinskitch agreed, turning the damaged gemstone over in his hands.

"*Oojipooka*," Oki murmured.

"What did you say?" Kendra asked.

"Oojipooka?" the little mouse replied uncertainly.

"I do say, I've never heard of such a word," Professor Bumblebean remarked, somewhat flustered.

"That's because Oki and I made it up," Ratchet declared. "Oki and I are going into the word-invention business. 'Oojipooka' is something you say when you are surprised by a mysterious object that can't be explained. Good job, Oki! You used the word perfectly!"

"You half-wit hairballs," Jinx groaned. "Who in their right mind would pay for a word?"

"I'm inclined to agree with our dear Jinx," Professor Bumblebean said. "Eens have thousands of words that they already employ. Furthermore, one can't just invent a word without submitting it for official scholarly scrutiny!"

"*Zoomba!*" Ratchet cried.

"What?" Kendra asked, not understanding either Ratchet or the Professor.

"HUMPH!" Uncle Griffinskitch grunted, tucking the ring behind his beard and glaring at the crew. "Enough of this nonsense."

Professor Bumblebean didn't look as if he wanted to let the matter drop—but then Agent Lurk sputtered awake and everyone turned to watch him.

It took a moment for the captured Een to collect his wits—but as soon as he did, he instinctively melted into invisibility. He quickly realized that he was tied up and reappeared.

"Fools!" Lurk screeched. "Let me go!"

"We don't take orders from you, *Agent Irk*," Jinx scowled. "And now we can finally see who's really hiding beneath your hood."

Lurk wriggled furiously in his binding, but there was no escape for him now. Jinx threw back his hood and at once Kendra felt her blood run cold. Agent Lurk looked like a picture of death and disease. His pale face was maimed and pocked with scars, and his head was so bald that he had not enough hair for even a single braid. One eye was dark and brooding, while the other was a vacant, milky white. He was a ghastly, terrifying sight to behold, but even so, it wasn't his deformity that startled Kendra so—it was his age.

Agent Lurk was a boy.

CHAPTER 4

The Face Beneath the Hood

You've probably had the experience of meeting someone for the first time and being completely surprised by what he or she looks like. It usually happens with a long-distance relative, someone you might have seen in a blurry old photograph or even talked to on the phone, but never actually met in person. Then, when you finally do see them, they turn out to be completely different from how you pictured it.

Such was the case with Agent Lurk. Even though Kendra had been chased by him all the way from the Land of Een, not once had she seen beneath his mysterious hood. His appearance had been left completely to her imagination—and what she had imagined was a man ancient as a tree.

How wrong she had been! Agent Lurk was no more than thirteen years old, scantly older than Kendra herself—yet he was deformed and desiccated.

"Wh-what happened to you?" she murmured.

"I don't need to answer you, girl," Agent Lurk sneered, seeming to relish the crew's reaction to his disfigurement. "I am my own master."

"My word!" Professor Bumblebean exclaimed. "You are clearly not an elder of Een, Leerlin Lurk. Surely, like every other good citizen of Een, you must answer to the Council of Elders."

"Ha!" Lurk chortled, a twinkle in his one good eye. "Then turn the ship around. Let us return to the Land of Een and submit ourselves to the mercy of the council."

"Humph," Uncle Griffinskitch grunted. "It is a dull game you play, boy. You know as well as I that the Land of Een is in shambles. Your own accomplice, Burdock Brown, rules the council like a king."

"The Land of Een is just as it should be," Lurk said. "I'm glad Burdock drove you and that old crone Winter Woodsong from the council."

"Aye," Uncle Griffinskitch growled. "Then a loyal subject ye shall make for 'King Burdock.'"

"I would rather live in Burdock's kingdom than by the rules of *your* council," Lurk hissed, but to Kendra's surprise, he wasn't directing the statement at her uncle. He seemed to be glaring right at *her*.

"Wh-wh-what?" Kendra stammered. "What did I do? I've never had any say on the council! I'm only twelve years old!"

Lurk's neck arched backwards as he unleashed a long and icy cackle. It was a strange and chilling sound; Kendra couldn't help but feel that there was a hint of pain and sadness in it. Yet when Lurk looked back at her, his one good eye was brimming red with hatred.

"Where is Kazah?" he demanded.

"I don't know, but that's a fantastic word," Ratchet declared. "Oki, maybe we should add it to our dictionary."

Oki peered out from behind Kendra's cloak, but could only manage a quiet eek.

Lurk scowled at the mouse. "Een critters—ridiculous to the last. In Burdock's land we shall be rid of your kind all together. Especially if I have anything to say about it."

"Is that so?" Jinx retorted. "Well, this is one Een critter that would happily pitch you over the side of the ship."

"Listen here, Kandlestar," Agent Lurk growled at Kendra. "Maybe you should learn to control these wild beasts you hold so dear to your heart. They need taming. Civilization. I can happily show you a few techniques."

"Eek!" Oki squealed.

Uncle Griffinskitch banged his staff against the floor. "HUMPH!" he boomed, and Kendra knew (much to her comfort) that it was the type of humph that meant he wasn't the least bit spooked by Agent Lurk. The old wizard walked a half circle in front of the boy, gazing at him intently. "What do you know of Kazah?" Uncle Griffinskitch asked after a moment.

"More than you," Lurk retaliated, gnashing his teeth. "Kazah is more powerful than you can imagine."

"I do say," Professor Bumblebean interjected. "I know most everything about the Land of Een and I have never heard of the power of Kazah."

"Not everything is in one of your books," Lurk sniggered. "At least not *yet*."

"Or in the books *you* know about," Uncle Griffinskitch told Agent Lurk as he reached into his beard and extracted the mysterious purple ring.

The effect on Agent Lurk was instantaneous. "Kazah!" he cried. He lurched forward, against the tug of his bindings, snarling so that Kendra could even see the gums above his teeth. At that moment he looked as dangerous as a wild beast, and it caused her to shudder. "You will give Kazah to me at once," Lurk demanded. "You can't possibly understand its power."

Professor Bumblebean adjusted his spectacles and leaned over to examine the cracked ring. "With such an egregious fracture, I doubt this tenebrous stone has any enchantment at all."

"Pompous windbag," Agent Lurk growled. "The crack *is* its power. I'm the one who discovered *that!* The crack in Kazah has allowed me a greater journey than you can ever imagine."

"My word!" Professor Bumblebean declared. "Whatever do you mean?"

But Agent Lurk ignored him. He turned back to Kendra and said, "Tell me, where is the Shard from Greeve? It must not be joined with the other fragments of the cauldron. Take the Shard—take it now—and throw it overboard."

"We can't," Ratchet said. "We don't even ha—,"

"Quiet your tongue, Ringtail!" Uncle Griffinskitch bellowed.

But it was too late. "Ah, I see," Agent Lurk said. "You don't have it—which means it's with the Unger. We must stop him from repairing the cauldron. Otherwise, I promise you this: the Land of Een, the one you so know and love, will perish."

"Humph," Uncle Griffinskitch muttered. "Should we love what the Land of Een has become under Burdock Brown?

Should we love watching the homes of innocent Eens burn? Should we love the comforts of a dungeon cell?"

"If it's for the greater good," Lurk replied.

"Then there is your folly," Uncle Griffinskitch retorted. "The greater is not always good."

With these final words, the wizard turned and shuffled out of the chamber.

"You just stay put," Jinx snarled at Lurk. Then she led Kendra and the rest of the crew from the compartment and shut the door behind them. They climbed the stairs to the deck, where Uncle Griffinskitch was ruminating over the ring.

"What now?" Kendra asked the old wizard.

"We continue forth," Uncle Griffinskitch said after a moment. "We shall find Kiro and unravel this mystery. Captain Ringtail, how much damage do you think the ship sustained during the skarm attack?"

"There's a few holes to patch up," Ratchet replied. "We need to find a place to berth so we can look her over."

"Very well," Uncle Griffinskitch said. "We'll make repairs—then onwards we go, to seek the City on the Storm."

Everyone set about to help prepare for the landing, yet Uncle Griffinskitch kept Kendra behind for a moment.

"What is it?" she asked.

"Kazah," the old wizard replied. "This ring . . . I think it is meant for your keeping."

"Why?" Kendra asked, giving her braids a startled tug.

Uncle Griffinskitch looked at her intently, as if carefully planning his words. "I have seen you wear it before," he said at last.

"What do you mean?" Kendra asked. "In a dream? When you were meditating?"

Uncle Griffinskitch shook his head, a mysterious look in his eyes. He placed the ring in her hand; it felt cold and heavy, but Kendra could feel no spark of magic.

"I don't know what I'm meant to do with this," she said.

"Humph," Uncle Griffinskitch muttered. It was a soft, quiet humph, one that Kendra couldn't even begin to decipher.

CHAPTER 5

Kendra and Oki Take a Tumble

It can be a strange wonder to inherit a family heirloom. Sometimes these things look so ancient and storied that there's just no way to fit them into our everyday lives. How can we wear our grandfather's antique pocket watch to school? Or our grandmother's silver pendant?

For Kendra, the Kazah Stone was extra troubling. Part of her was excited and proud that Uncle Griffinskitch had entrusted the ring to her; yet just to look at it left a queasy feeling in her stomach. After all, it was Agent Lurk's. What if the Kazah Stone had maimed him? What if it was the thing that had turned him so wicked? Kendra had already tried to wrestle with the terrible power of the Shard from Greeve; as far as she was concerned, she had had her fill of dark magic.

Such thoughts were turning in her mind when Ratchet suddenly cried, "I've found it! The perfect port."

Kendra tucked the ring into her pocket and hurried over to the railing with the rest of the crew. Ratchet was maneuvering the *Big Bang* alongside a steep cliff face.

"There's no place to land here," Kendra murmured, but then she saw a small ledge of rock tucked behind an outcropping of trees.

"We'll be safe from prying eyes here," Ratchet surmised.

Oki pulled a cord to shrink the ship's balloon, and as the *Big Bang* began to descend, Ratchet released the landing gear, which consisted of two long spindly legs. In a moment the giant, bird-like ship came to a perch on the snowy rocks.

"You know, I think we're near the Land of Een," said Ratchet as he began casting lines to secure the ship.

"Aye," Uncle Griffinskitch murmured. "Unfortunately, it's not Een we're trying to find."

"I do say," Professor Bumblebean chimed in, "if we are near Een, then we are also in the vicinity of the Crags of Dredge, the nesting place of the skarm."

"If that's the case, then we must make haste in our repairs," Uncle Griffinskitch said.

The ship, however, was more severely damaged than Ratchet had first estimated. The balloon needed patching and the hull had been gashed open in two places, which meant it took the crew well into the evening to complete the repairs. Even so, Uncle Griffinskitch was against spending the night on the ledge, and so they set forth again across the winter skies.

"She sails like a charm," Ratchet cried from the helm. "*Foogiewunda!*"

"What does that mean?" Kendra asked.

"It means 'hooray,'" the raccoon explained.

"Then why not just say hooray?" Jinx asked irritably.

"Because it's not half as much fun as saying *foogiewunda*!" Ratchet replied.

The raccoon and grasshopper were soon embroiled in a furious debate. Kendra, too weary to listen, trudged below-decks to the cabin she shared with Oki.

The little mouse was already fast asleep in his hammock, but Kendra left the candle lit for a little longer. She sat on the edge of her bunk, feeling too tired to even take off her boots. Then she remembered Kazah. She took out the mysterious ring and turned it over in her hands. She stared into its deep fracture. She couldn't help thinking of Agent Lurk's words: *"I would rather live in Burdock's kingdom than by the rules of your council."*

Why had he said that? It was like he knew something she did not. Her mind was dizzy with thoughts.

Still holding the Kazah Stone, Kendra closed her eyes for a moment and breathed deeply. There was a game she used to play when she was little, when she felt panicked or over-whelmed. She would imagine her family, what they would have looked like, what it would have felt like to know them. Especially, she would think about her mother, the infamous Kayla Kandlestar. Trying to imagine her always helped Kendra forget her worries.

Everyone had always said that Kayla Kandlestar was a skilled sorceress. She was legendary for her wild and impetuous behavior. Burdock Brown had especially hated her—but that was no big surprise. That hunched and horrid old wizard hated pretty much everyone. But most Eens would just look away uncomfortably when the subject of Kendra's mother came up. Those were Eens for you; they even had a saying: "If you can't say something nice, pretend your tongue is ice."

Just what had her mother done to upset everyone so much? Back at home, there was a painting or two of Kayla hanging on the walls. Kendra tried to imagine them now. It had been so long since she had been home. She missed those walls! She missed those pictures. She tried to remember one particular portrait of her mother that was in the kitchen hanging next to the narfoo, that complicated musical instrument. Kendra tried to use Uncle Griffinskitch's model of meditation, concocting in her mind every detail of her mother. She imagined the color of her hair and eyes, the blush of her cheek. She tried to imagine her mother's voice, and what it might have felt like to hold her hand. She even tried to imagine her smell . . .

"Kendra! What's happening?"

It was Oki. The little mouse was squeaking frantically and tugging at her sleeve. Kendra opened her eyes, only to find the room a complete blur. Everything seemed to be spinning around her—were they under attack again?

"The ring—it's glowing!" Oki exclaimed.

Kendra still couldn't see—but she could feel. Kazah, clutched tight in her hands, was throbbing with warmth.

"Oki!" Kendra cried.

"I'm here—I won't let go of you! EEK!"

Suddenly it was bright. And cold. To her horror, Kendra realized she and Oki were outside, hurtling through the sky, towards the ground.

"What's happening?!" Kendra shrieked.

"I don't know," Oki squealed, "but we better do something!"

Kendra's wand was tucked in her belt. Desperately, she reached for it with her free hand, still clutching the Kazah Stone in her other.

Concentrate, she told herself. Even though she was terrified and falling, she found a pocket of calm and clarity in one corner of her mind. She seized onto this and chanted:

Wand of might,
Ease our flight;
Like a sprite,
Let us alight.

It was hardly the best spell in the world, but she kept repeating it and soon enough they began to slow down. Kendra could see the landscape rise up around them: mountains, crags, and hills. Soon Kendra could see the trees; they were now approaching them at what felt like an alarming speed.

"We're still falling too fast!" Oki squealed. "Try to slow—,"

Crack! They struck the top of a tree—heavily—and tumbled through its network of branches, snapping twigs and sending down a shower of leaves as they fell. Kendra wasn't about to let her wand slip from her grasp for a second time in one day; she gripped it tightly—but the Kazah Stone rolled from her hand and fell through the branches towards the ground.

Kendra felt a branch rake across her face and another jab into her ribs. Then she finally came to a stop, landing on her back against a thin bough that bent, but did not break. Oki ended up right on top of her. For a minute they just lay there, trying to collect their wits.

"Are you okay?" Oki asked eventually.

Kendra nodded, carefully sliding her wand into her belt. "You?"

Oki managed a weak smile. "What happened?"

Kendra shook her head, confused. "I'm not sure. Where are we? Why is everything so green? There shouldn't be leaves on this tree; it's the middle of winter!"

But it wasn't winter. Even though she didn't dare sit up (she was worried the branch would break), Kendra could see that the sky had changed from dismal gray to blazing blue. She could feel the heat in the air, smell the fragrance of moss and ferns. She could hear the hoot and caw of forest birds.

She could also hear a voice. It came from below, with a threat: "What's going on up there? You want to attack me? Just bring it on, slurpburgers! I'll zap you into next week!"

"Eek!" Oki squealed, at the same time giving a little jump—and this was all it took for their branch to snap. Down they went again, crashing through the bottommost boughs of the tree. They never really hit the ground; instead they landed right on top of whoever had spoken, ending up in a tangle of arms and legs at the base of the trunk. Finally, after a few seconds of grunting and groaning, everyone was able to stand and look at each other.

"Holy hooglegum!" Oki cried.

Standing before them was a Teenling—an Een girl no more than fifteen years old. And she looked remarkably like Kendra.

CHAPTER 6

The Wild Girl in the Woods

For a moment, Kendra was so stunned that she couldn't speak. Staring at the girl's face was like looking into a mirror. They shared the same eyes, the same nose, even the same mouth.

But the similarities ended there. Not only was the girl older (and taller) than Kendra, she had a wild look about her, as if at any moment she might lift her chin and howl like an Unger. Her hair was a mess, tousled and tangled with beaded braids that jutted out in a mishmash of directions like snakes trying to wriggle free of an unkempt nest. She was adorned head to foot with bangles and baubles, and her robe, sky blue in color, hung off one shoulder in a way that Kendra thought was just a little too carefree—at least for a sorceress.

And a sorceress the girl certainly was (or at least an apprentice), for now she raised a slender wand of Eenwood and brandished it before Kendra and Oki like it was a weapon.

"I thought you were Goojuns," the girl said in a sharp, accusatory tone. "What are you doing messing around out here? You trying to trick me? How did you get up that tree?"

"Eek!" Oki whimpered. "You ask a lot of questions."

"Then let's just start with one, *Eeks,*" the Teenling snapped, pointing her wand at Oki. "You got a name?"

"Er . . . his name is Oki," Kendra said, stepping forward with as much boldness as she could muster. "And I'm Kendra."

"Hmph," the girl grunted, looking Kendra up and down. "Nice braids," she said in a sarcastic tone. "Someone zap you with his wand?"

"No!" Kendra said indignantly.

"Hmph," the Teenling muttered, circling them and tapping one long finger against her Eenwood. "You look familiar, *Braids,*" she said after a moment. "You got a last name?"

"Kandlestar?" Kendra said uncertainly. She suddenly found her confidence melting as she spoke. This Teenling was strong and bold and—in a wild sort of way—beautiful too. For a reason she couldn't quite explain, Kendra wanted to impress her.

But she clearly wasn't off to a good start. "Kandlestar?" the Teenling muttered, wrinkling her nose as if Kendra's name somehow came with a rotten smell. "You're not related to that Krimson fellow, are you? What a snorehog! Always tinkering in his garden or quoting some monotonous Een legend. BOR-ing!"

Kendra and Oki looked at each other in surprise. Krimson Kandlestar was the name of Kendra's father, but he had disappeared along with Kendra's mother and brother, eleven years ago. *How could this Teenling remember my father?* Kendra wondered. *She must have been just a toddler when he disappeared.* Kendra gave her braids a fretful tug and began to ask, "Did you know—,"

"How did you get way up that tree?" the girl interrupted, repeating her earlier question. "You can't just fall from the sky."

"Well . . . ," Kendra murmured. The truth was they *had* fallen from the sky—but Kendra wasn't even sure how. One minute she had been looking at the Kazah Stone and the next—"Oh!" Kendra exclaimed, suddenly remembering that she had dropped the ring. *It must have landed somewhere around here,* Kendra thought, frantically dropping to her knees to search the canopy of ferns and flowers.

"What are you looking for?" the girl demanded.

"Kazah!" Kendra answered, crawling through the undergrowth. "My ring!"

"You dropped it?" Oki cried, joining Kendra on the ground. "Oh, dear!"

"Ring? What ring?" the Teenling asked, looming over them. "What's so special about it?"

"My master gave it to me," Kendra said over her shoulder. "It's . . . er, important." She didn't want to tell the girl too much. After all, Kendra herself wasn't exactly sure what to make of the Kazah Stone.

"Well, I didn't see anything," the Teenling said, shuffling after Kendra and Oki as they crawled across the forest floor. "If you dropped it from that tree, it could have bounced away anywhere. Even down some hole."

"But we have to find it!" Kendra said.

"Not now we don't, Braids," the girl said, reaching down and pulling Kendra to her feet. "With all the racket you two

Eeklings made crashing through that tree, it's a wonder the flysuckers aren't already here."

"Eek! Flysuckers?" Oki asked, looking about nervously.

"Yeah, you know—Goojuns," the girl replied. "We *are* in the Forests of Wretch, after all."

"EEK!" Oki squealed. "The Forests of Wretch!? Don't think of eggs! Don't think of eggs!"

"Eggs?" the Teenling echoed. "You know what, Eeks? You're a strange little ball of whiskers."

"But the Forests of Wretch!" Oki exclaimed, his eyes going wide. "That's close to Goojun City!"

"Yeah, we're practically in their backyard," the girl proclaimed proudly. "That's why we have to get going."

Kendra fussed with her longest braid, shaking her head. "But the ring—,"

"Look, Braids," the Teenling said, turning to Kendra. "We can always come back for it if we need to. Don't worry. I'm sure it will turn up."

Before Kendra could argue the matter any further, the girl turned and began marching briskly through the forest. Kendra cast a weary glance at Oki. The Teenling was nearly out of sight already. She hadn't even bothered to turn and check if they were following.

"That's one *jinxly* Teenling," Oki observed.

Kendra raised an eyebrow at the little mouse. "Jinx isn't going to appreciate you making up new words based on her," Kendra told Oki. "But you're right . . . this girl *is* . . . er, jinxly. But what do we do? It's either her or the Goojuns."

"Her," Oki said quickly. "And, if you ask me, I think she took the Kazah Stone."

"Why would she do that?" Kendra exclaimed.

"I don't know," Oki said. "But if I'm right, it's all the more reason to stick with her."

"Come on then," Kendra said, clutching Oki's paw. "Er . . . miss?" she panted as they hastened to catch up with the Teenling. "Wait up!"

"Miss?" the girl snarled, still not turning around.

"Well . . . we don't know your name," Kendra said.

"Gayla."

Gayla. The name fluttered across Kendra's mind like a bird seeking a place to land. Why was that name so familiar? She looked down at Oki, but he only shrugged.

She turned back to Gayla. "Where are we going?" Kendra asked.

"Gotta get home," Gayla said, not even bothering to look at Kendra when she spoke. "Beards is going to be hotter than a hairball when he realizes I snuck out again."

"Beards? Who's that?" Kendra asked.

"My master," Gayla replied curtly.

"So we're going to Een?" Oki asked.

"No kidding, Eeks," Gayla retorted. "That's where Eens live. Well, me, anyway. I'm not sure what universe you two fluster-busters come from."

"But how do we get past the magic curtain?" Kendra asked, fiddling with one braid.

Gayla turned, looked down at them and made a face. "You two bump your heads on the way down that tree?"

Kendra looked at her blankly.

"We walk through it," Gayla explained irritably. "Just like we always do. Isn't that how you pair of moaning miracles ended up out here? Hmph. I figured you were different from those worry-winks who sit around Een fretting about the outside world. Or did you just get lost on your way to school?"

"We're not in school!" Kendra cried. "We're apprentices."

"She knows that," Oki said. "She's just being jinxly again."

"Hmph," Gayla muttered, and she set off through the forest once more.

Kendra let her take a few strides ahead then turned and whispered to Oki, "Burdock sealed the curtain! How are we supposed to get through without his spell?"

"I don't know," Oki said. "It's like Een has completely changed since we've been gone."

"We've been away for months," Kendra mused. "Do you think Burdock stepped down? Maybe Winter Woodsong is running things again."

"Maybe," Oki murmured thoughtfully. "But how did the weather change so suddenly? One minute it's snowing and the next it's summer!"

"What are you two whispering about?" Gayla snapped over her shoulder.

"Er . . . nothing," Kendra said. She cast one more sidelong glance at Oki. He didn't say anything, but he didn't need to. Kendra was thinking the exact same thing: *Something strange is going on here. And I have no idea what it is.*

CHAPTER 7

A Journey to When

If you have ever tried to seek the Land of Een, then you know it is a near-impossible quest. You would certainly need one of the small folk from that tiny place to guide you, for it is Eens alone who can cross the magic curtain. Why, if you or I tried to step through it, we would just end up on the other side of the Land of Een, none the wiser. For Eens, of course, it's different. As soon as *they* step through the curtain they will feel a slight crackle in the air, a tingle on the skin—and then they will be safely home.

Of course, the last time Kendra had crossed the curtain it had taken powerful magic. This was because Burdock Brown had sealed the curtain to prevent anyone from coming or

45

going. Indeed, as Gayla now led them towards the curtain, Kendra half-expected to find it still blocked. Yet the plucky Teenling did not hesitate at all. She stepped through the curtain as simply as one walks through the rain. It was just like the "old days" (as Ratchet would say), before Burdock came to power.

"Strange," Kendra mumbled.

"Talking about yourself again?" Gayla snickered, turning to confront Kendra.

"No," Kendra said. She realized at once it was a weak comeback, so she quickly changed the subject by asking, "Where are we exactly?"

"The Hills of Wight," Gayla replied. "Isn't it the way you two came?"

"Well, er . . . ," Kendra murmured.

"Getting an answer out of you two tree-tumblers is harder than getting a laugh from an Unger," Gayla growled in exasperation. "Look, just tell me which way you're headed."

Kendra cast Oki a perplexed look. "Home?" she whispered. "To the yew tree house? Or maybe we should go to your parents."

"And share a bed with my eight sisters?" Oki squeaked. "No thanks! Besides—Burdock has declared us criminals, remember? I don't want to get my family in trouble."

"But if the curtain's open now, Burdock can't be ruling anymore," Kendra said.

"What's up with you two murmuring measles?" Gayla demanded. "Don't you ever have a normal conversation? You know, *out loud?*"

"Er . . . sorry," Kendra said. "We were just trying to decide where to go."

"How about home?" Gayla suggested, crossing her arms. "You do have a home, don't you?"

"Well . . . we lived with my uncle," Kendra replied.

"What do you mean *lived?*" Gayla demanded. "And what about your parents?"

Kendra struggled for a reply and instead just tugged nervously on her braids. How come this girl didn't know that her parents had disappeared? She claimed to know Krimson, and if that was true then she should know that he was gone. After all, it seemed to Kendra that *everyone* in Faun's End knew about her family disappearing. It had made Kendra herself sort of famous, just by default. She had never enjoyed that notoriety, of course, but now it sort of annoyed her that this wild Een girl was so oblivious to everything. Then again, Kendra couldn't help wondering why she had never heard of Gayla before. She wasn't exactly hard to notice. On market day in Faun's End she would stick out like a smile on Uncle Griffinskitch.

"Oh, I get it," Gayla said after Kendra's hesitation. "You're an orphan."

Kendra yanked on one of her braids and managed only a nod.

"Hmph," Gayla grunted. "Don't sweat it, Braids. So am I."

"You are?" Kendra asked.

"Yeah," Gayla replied with a wave of her arms. "No big deal. I live with my brother. C'mon, just follow me. We live just outside of Faun's End."

Without waiting for further discussion, she turned on one heel and set across the low hills that rolled before them.

"We better keep an eye out for Burdock and his men," Kendra told Oki quietly. "Just in case they're still looking for us."

"You're whispering again!" Gayla accused over her shoulder.

Fiddling with her braids, Kendra decided it was best to keep quiet and see if she could make it three steps without rousing Gayla's ire.

They walked for a few hours, for we must remember that Een feet are small and their destination lay some distance from the curtain. Yet with each step the landscape grew more familiar, and by mid-afternoon Kendra realized with sudden elation that their path would take them right past the old yew tree house where she lived with Uncle Griffinskitch.

They turned a bend and Kendra's heart leapt as her home came into sight. It was a strange house to be sure, the trunk of a yew tree rising above its roof. In fact, the house was built right into the tree, and here and there doors or windows peered out between roots or from a knothole in the bark, giving a tantalizing hint of the mysterious rooms that lay beyond. It was a true wizard's home, filled with nooks and crannies and odd, confusing passages. Kendra adored it.

Yet something was now different about the house. At first Kendra couldn't put her finger on it, but as they drew closer she realized the house looked to be in fantastic condition. In fact, it looked better than it ever had.

Strange, Kendra thought as they walked along the fenced pathway that circled the house. *It's been months since we've been here.*

Yet here were some fresh flowers planted outside the front door (something she had never seen before), and the windows had been cleaned (her own chore, one she often neglected). Then Kendra noticed a trickle of smoke curling out from the kitchen chimney. She stopped and stared.

"Someone's moved into my house!" she exclaimed. Her stomach was churning with both anger and fear; if anyone has ever come into your room and meddled with your belongings while you were away, then you probably know exactly how Kendra was feeling at this moment.

"Eek!" Oki cried. "I bet it's Captain Rinkle!"

"What are you two nattering ninnies mumbling about now?" Gayla demanded. "This is *my* house. Or my brother's, if you want to get all professor about it. Which old Beards would. He's kind of annoying that way. Master *and* brother."

Kendra turned and looked at Gayla. *Master and brother?* she thought—and then a realization struck her. It was like a hammer ringing a bell; for at that very moment she knew why Gayla's name sounded so familiar—and it made her feel faint.

"What's wrong, Braids?" Gayla asked. "You look like you've seen an Unger."

The Kazah Stone, Kendra thought. *It's taken us . . .* Her knees began to wobble. "G-G-Gayla?" Kendra stammered. "Your name is Gayla? And your master is your brother? Master . . . "

"Gregor," Gayla said brusquely. "Gregor Griffinskitch. You probably know him. He's always parading about, trying to get on the council and sucking up to all the Eld . . . "

But Kendra didn't hear the rest. For now it was perfectly clear to her, and it was at once both terrifying and magnificent. It wasn't *where* they had landed, Kendra realized, but *when*. Somehow she and Oki had traveled back through time—and they had found her mother.

CHAPTER 8

Uncle Griffinskitch Comes Home

In your time as a young adventurer, following Kendra's many quests, you have probably come to learn a great deal about the magical race of Eens. Certainly you have realized that they have a rather sing-song quality to their names, with the sounds of their first matching their last. Take, for example, the name of our young heroine, Kendra Kandlestar, or the names of a few of her friends: Ratchet Ringtail, Honest Oki, and Juniper Jinx.

Indeed, names are very important to Eens—so much so that they will change them, *both* first and last, when they marry, just to keep this magical sound alive. Sometimes it's the wife that will change her names, sometimes the husband. It doesn't really matter to Eens, as long as they can keep that sing-song sound. In the case of

Kendra's family, it was her mother who had made the change, but it had been something that Kendra had completely forgotten—until now.

"Your mom wasn't always called Kayla Kandlestar, you know," Ratchet had told Kendra one day while she watched him tinker with one of his inventions. "She only changed her name to match your father when they married. The way my gramps tells it, your uncle was furious. Gramps says he yelled so loud that it shook the magic curtain."

"Why? What made him so angry?" Kendra remembered asking.

"I guess he thought the Griffinskitch name was better," was Ratchet's explanation. "According to Gramps, your mom was becoming this great sorceress, while your dad was just a simple gardener. If anything, your uncle thought your dad should do the old name switcheroo. But your mom refused. She changed her name and waved good-bye to the name of Gayla Griffinskitch."

And now, young readers, you will understand why this name had seemed vaguely familiar to Kendra. Her mind had fumbled with it until this very moment, when at last she had pieced together the puzzle to realize that the wild Teenling who stood before her was her mother—or at least the girl who would one day become her mother.

Yet she was hardly what Kendra had expected. The person Kendra had always imagined (and you too, no doubt) was loving and nurturing. This girl, Gayla Griffinskitch, was obnoxious, wild—and maybe even a thief!

It was too much for Kendra to think about all at once. Her legs felt weak and her stomach began to churn. Oki squeaked at her, but it sounded as if his voice was far away. The whole world began to spin around her—then, in one fell swoop, she fainted.

When Kendra came to, she found herself stretched out on one of the big wooden chairs in the kitchen of the yew tree house. Near her, on the hearth, a small cauldron was bubbling. It offered a comforting, familiar smell. Countless times Kendra had leaned over that cauldron, preparing dinner for her and Uncle Griffinskitch, and for a moment she managed to convince herself that everything that had happened that day was just a muddled dream.

Somehow I fell out of the cloud ship and banged my head, she thought. *And now, here I am, safe inside my own house. I didn't really meet . . .*

Then Gayla leaned over her. "Hmph," she snorted. "You're alive after all. I told Eeks you'd be okay." She dabbed at Kendra's forehead with a ball of cloth—and instinctively Kendra jerked away. She couldn't help it—meeting this young version of her mother was all too strange. It was like encountering a ghost.

"Don't worry, Braids," Gayla said hotly. "I'm not going to hurt you. Who do you think carried you all the way in here?"

Kendra's mind was buzzing. She found herself wanting to do one of two things. The first was to hug Gayla and tell her that she was her daughter. The second was to run out the door and try to forget any of this had ever happened. But in truth, Kendra was too stunned to do either.

"Besides," Gayla continued, completely oblivious to Kendra's swirling vortex of emotions, "you're not going to get any nursing from Beards. Or sympathy."

"Uncle Griffinskitch?" Kendra murmured.

"He's not my uncle," the Teenling said. "I told you, he's my brother."

Kendra's eyes flickered. Everything was so confusing! "Oki?" Kendra murmured.

"He's out picking carrots for the soup," Gayla replied. "But he wouldn't say what's going on with you two. I guess that's *your* job." She crossed her arms and looked at Kendra expectantly.

"Well, er . . ." Kendra stammered. She had no idea what to say. Instead she just stared at the floor.

"Let me guess," Gayla finally said. "You have an ornery old master who treats you like kitchen scraps. So you filched his ring and ran for the hills. And then you bump into me and now you have no place to go."

"That . . . er, sounds about right," Kendra said. *At least the part about having no place to go,* she added in her head.

"You can stay here for now," Gayla said, turning to stir the soup on the hearth. "Beards won't like it—but he doesn't like anything. What happened to your folks anyway?"

"They were lost," Kendra said, tugging nervously on one braid. "Outside the curtain."

"Oh," Gayla said matter-of-factly. "Did you know them?"

"N-no," Kendra said. "I was just a baby."

"Yeah, never knew my parents either," Gayla declared. "My mom died when I was born—she was pretty old, you know. Then my dad died right afterwards. Broken heart, Beards says. Whatever. Now it's just me and him."

Kendra was in shock. She had spent her whole life without parents, but it had never occurred to her that her own mother had grown up the same way.

"But Unc—Beards, I mean, your brother, that is," Kendra sputtered. "He's your brother. He cares about you."

"Hmph," Gayla muttered with a roll of her eyes. "You've obviously never met him! He was thirty years old when I was born. Sure, most Een siblings have large gaps between them—but not *that* large. My brother never expected to have a sister, especially one he'd have to take care of."

Kendra tugged a braid. This story sounded all too familiar.

"The only thing Beards cares about is becoming an elder," Gayla continued. "That's why we have to always act like model citizens. Set the right example. Een forbid we ever damage his reputation—or his chance of becoming an elder."

At that moment, as if to catch Gayla in the act of speaking ill of him, the door flew open and there stood Uncle Griffin-skitch himself. Or at least Kendra was sure it must be him. The uncle she knew was mostly one long white beard and so hunched and squat that he was a full head shorter than her.

This Uncle Griffinskitch was actually taller than her, an imposing fellow with a gray beard that barely went past his waist.
He was wearing a dark robe, and in his hand he was holding
a wide-brimmed hat with a long, crooked peak. Kendra had
never imagined that Uncle Griffinskitch could look so young
and vital. Indeed, she might not have recognized him at all,
except for his eyes—and his voice.

"HUMPH!" he scowled. "And who is this?"

Kendra assumed he was speaking about her, but he reached
behind him and pushed forth little Oki, who looked more
abashed than ever.

"He was racing through the garden like a wild Izzard,"
Uncle Griffinskitch grouched. "Scurried right into me, not
even looking where he was going." Then the wizard noticed
Kendra sitting next to the fire. "Another one! Who—,"

"Relax," Gayla interjected, rolling her eyes. "These are my
friends."

"Humph," Uncle Griffinskitch muttered. "I suppose I
should be pleased that someone wants to come around here
other than that Krimson boy, but—,"

"He planted all the flowers around the front door," Gayla
interrupted. "You said they brightened the place up."

"Aye," Uncle Griffinskitch muttered, hanging his hat on a
hook by the door. "As I was about to say—you're a little old to
be playing with Eenlings."

"They're not Eenlings—look, she's got a wand," Gayla
said, pointing at Kendra.

"Humph," Uncle Griffinskitch grumbled, casting the
most fleeting of glances in Kendra's direction. His voice and
glare were so dismissive that Kendra shrank into her chair. She
wished she could just disappear. Thankfully, Oki slipped

across the room and climbed into the chair next to her, which instantly made her feel better.

"I told you last week they were coming," Gayla said to Uncle Griffinskitch. "Remember? They've come all the way from Charlo's Crook for Jamboreen. It's tomorrow!"

Kendra looked at Oki in surprise and excitement. Jamboreen was the biggest festival in the Land of Een, a grand carnival held every year on the longest day of the year. Of course, Kendra hadn't looked at a calendar since arriving in the past; to discover that Jamboreen was the very next day sent a thrill to the very tips of her pointed ears. It would be like you suddenly waking up one day and instead of having to go to school you were told it was Christmas vacation.

Uncle Griffinskitch frowned at Kendra. "Who's your master, child?"

Kendra tugged nervously at her braids. How could she tell him that it was, well . . . *him?*

"It's Nevryn Nightsky," Gayla piped up.

"Never heard of him," Uncle Griffinskitch muttered.

"Hmph," Gayla grunted. "I guess you don't know everything."

Kendra stifled a gasp. She would never dare speak to Uncle Griffinskitch in such a manner. She watched the old Een's ears turn red (a sure sign that he was angry), but all he said was, "I'm in no mood for your Eenling ways today."

"Good thing I'm not an Eenling then," Gayla retorted.

"Humph—you might have fooled me," Uncle Griffinskitch growled.

Gayla just glared at him. Then, thrusting her spoon into the soup pot, she turned and snatched the narfoo from its peg on the wall.

That instrument is hers? Kendra thought in amazement.

"Where do you think you're going?" Uncle Griffinskitch demanded.

Gayla didn't answer. Instead, she brushed past him and disappeared out the front door.

A moment later, the sound of her narfoo could be heard emanating from the front garden. Her tune was a complicated one, layered with rich textures and sounds. To Kendra the song sounded angry and woeful at the same time.

Uncle Griffinskitch glared after his sister. Then, turning and striding across the kitchen, he took a seat at the hearth, right across from Kendra and Oki.

He still has his favorite chair, Kendra thought. *Or I suppose it was his favorite chair and still will be in the future. Oh, it's all so confusing!* She looked up at the cantankerous wizard and flashed him a weak smile.

"Humph," he grunted. Then he promptly closed his eyes and began to snore.

CHAPTER 9

A Conundrum of Time

There's nothing worse than being in an uncomfortable situation in someone else's house. You can't just quietly sneak off to your room; really, the best you can do is to just politely excuse yourself and leave. Of course, in a way, Kendra was already at home—she and Oki had no place else to go.

So, instead, Kendra did as she had countless times before: she made dinner for Uncle Griffinskitch. Oki helped her, and when it was ready they called Gayla and the crotchety wizard to the table. Uncle Griffinskitch sputtered awake, but Gayla ignored the summons altogether and simply continued playing her narfoo in the front garden. When Kendra suggested she fetch her, Uncle Griffinskitch only humphed. It was the type of humph Kendra knew all too well: it meant *leave it be*. So it was just Kendra, Oki, and Uncle Griffinskitch at the table and there they sat, without the slightest word between them. Not that they would have heard each other anyway, for Gayla played her narfoo so raucously that Kendra couldn't hear the slurp of her own soup. She was sure the racket was meant to irk Uncle Griffinskitch, but if he was perturbed, he didn't show it. Indeed, he barely looked up from his dinner.

Days of Een, Kendra thought. *The uncle I know is merry as the River Wink compared to this curmudgeon.*

After dinner, Uncle Griffinskitch disappeared up the stairs (to his study, Kendra presumed), leaving Kendra and Oki to tidy up.

It was the first time the two friends had been given a chance to talk in private since their arrival at the house, and they instantly began speaking in hushed whispers.

"We've traveled through time, Kendra," Oki squealed.

"I kind of figured it out," she replied. "It was the Kazah Stone—that much is obvious. Remember? Lurk said it took him on a great journey."

"Then where is Lurk from?" Oki wondered. "Or should I say *when*? It gives me the shivers just thinking about it."

"I know," Kendra said. She carried the dinner bowls over to the washtub, which was overflowing with dirty dishes. *Someone hasn't done this job in a while,* she thought. She began to pump the water and found her gaze wandering out the window, where she could see Gayla sitting on a large toadstool, a dark and wild figure against the rising moon. She was still playing her narfoo, but her tune had turned solemn and woeful.

"I can't believe that's my mother," Kendra said after a moment. "She's not exactly the kindest person I've ever met. She called Krimson—well, er . . . my dad—a bore!"

"I think she just says things like that," Oki said. "She's tough on the outside, but on the inside I think she's all *ishy-moosha*."

Kendra raised an eyebrow.

"It means soft and sentimental," Oki explained.

"Maybe you're right," Kendra said. Then, after a pause, she added, "Do you think I should tell her who I am? That I'm from the future? That I'm her daughter?"

"NO!" Oki squealed. "You can't do that, Kendra. That would be . . . disastrous!"

"Why?" Kendra asked.

"We don't belong here!" Oki exclaimed, throwing his paws in the air. "Remember when Ratchet was inventing his time boots, the ones that never ended up working? He said you

61

have to be careful with time travel. You can't go fiddling with the timeline. If you change something in the past it could change the future."

"What if it's a good change?" Kendra countered. "What if we warn Gayla about what's going to happen? Maybe she won't run away from Een with my family! Maybe Kiro will never become Trooogul!"

"Or maybe everything turns out far worse," Oki argued. "We could all be captured by a witch and transformed into spotted eggs."

"I wouldn't mind that for Burdock," Kendra mused. "I'd crack him."

"We don't know what might happen," Oki insisted. "If you tell Gayla that you're her daughter, she probably won't even believe you! What if she decides to do the opposite of what you tell her is going to happen just to be stubborn? She might never marry your father. You'd never be born! Then what's going to happen to you? You might just suddenly vanish into thin air!"

"You're making my head hurt," Kendra said, tugging extra hard on a braid.

"That's the trouble with time travel," Oki said. "It's one big ball of confusion. A real *hooglegum*."

"We have to get Kazah back, Oki," Kendra said. "It's the only way we can get back to the right time. Otherwise we're stuck here."

"Well, my parents aren't born in this time yet," Oki said thoughtfully, "which means I don't have any annoying sisters here either . . . "

"You're the one who was just fretting about the timeline," Kendra pointed out.

"I know, I know," Oki said. "We have to find the ring."

They had been talking so intently that they had failed to notice that the music had stopped and now—suddenly—Gayla was standing in the room. She had quietly slipped inside to catch the tail end of their conversation.

"What are you two dish-diddling dewberries mumbling about now?" Gayla asked, hanging her narfoo back on the wall. "Why do you keep fretting about this ring?"

Kendra turned to face Gayla, her cheeks burning red. She felt as if she had been caught in the moment of telling a secret—and those of us familiar with Kendra's past adventures know her feelings about secrets. She had experienced enough problems with them to fill a lifetime. The difference now was that Kendra *wanted* to tell the truth—but she couldn't. And so she stammered, "I t-told you already. It's just important."

Gayla glared at her suspiciously. "Why is it important? What aren't you telling me, Braids?"

Oki gave a quiet eek and Kendra cast him a frown.

"Hmph," Gayla muttered. "You're a real pair of sneaky snirtles. I tell you what—cough up what's so special about this ring and I'll help you find it."

"We don't need your help," Kendra said quickly.

"Sure," Gayla said. "You're going to find it yourselves, are you? In the Forests of Wretch? You're just lucky I was there today! Otherwise, you'd both be Goojun snacks."

"Eek!" Oki squealed again, clinging to Kendra's leg. "Oh, don't think of eggs!"

"You know, Eeks, you're a real worry-whisker," Gayla growled, shaking a fist at the little mouse. "And you're beginning to get on my nerves."

"Leave him alone!" Kendra shouted. "Why do you always have to be so mean?"

"Why do you have to be so annoying?" Gayla demanded. "I didn't ask you to come here! You dropped on *my* head, remember?"

"Then just give me back my ring and we'll get out of your way," Kendra said, giving one of her braids a strong tug.

Gayla took a long, slow step forward. "What did you say?" she demanded, crossing her arms.

Kendra glared at her.

"If you want to accuse me of something, just come out and say it," Gayla uttered.

Kendra gulped, and tried to collect her courage. "D-did you take it? Did you take my ring?"

Gayla stared her straight in the eye. "No," she said finally, her voice calm and even. And with that, she turned on one heel and stormed up the stairs.

Kendra realized she had been holding her breath and let out a long exhale. She turned and looked down at Oki. "What now?" she asked, suddenly realizing that a single hot tear was trickling down her cheek. "Do you think she's lying?"

"I don't know," Oki said quietly. "But if she is, she's really good at it."

CHAPTER 10
The Great Jamboreen

There is no festival in the world quite like Jamboreen. If you are ever so lucky as to find yourself at this marvelous celebration, I imagine it will be one of the best days of your life. Here you will find Eens dressed in colorful costumes, wearing masks or painted faces, and walking on long stilts, juggling glowing balls or performing tricks. You will taste the most delicious treats: Eenberry pie, honey trifles, and roasted acorns glazed with Een sugar. You will hear silly songs, dance to jubilant music, and play the strangest games you can imagine. Indeed, each and every minute will bring a new spectacle, and the revelry will last into the wee hours of the night, until at last you collapse in a heap of happy exhaustion.

It can be no surprise that Jamboreen was Kendra's favorite day of the year. On this particular morning, however, she awoke stiff, sore, and sour as a skarm. She was still upset about her fight with Gayla, and to make matters worse, no one had bothered to show her and Oki a bed, so they had spent the night curled up on hard wooden chairs. Needless to say, it had been an uncomfortable sleep.

"This just might turn out to be the worst Jamboreen ever," Kendra groaned.

These words had no sooner left her lips when there came from upstairs the sound of someone singing. The voice was so beautiful and melodic that it caused Kendra's neck to prickle with goose bumps.

"Wh-who is that?" Kendra murmured.

"Definitely not your uncle," Oki declared.

It was Gayla, of course. Singing all the way, she danced down the stairs and swept into the kitchen, the perfect picture of a splendid mood. It was as if she had completely forgotten the events from the night before. Her hair was now streaked purple and blue, with large bulbs and stars hanging from her braids, and she was wearing a beautiful robe the color of a summer's night.

"It's Jamboreen!" she announced with a trill in her voice.

Kendra and Oki exchanged looks of bewilderment, but for once, Gayla didn't seem to notice. With a twirl and a song, she ushered them to separate bathtubs. By the time Kendra had finished washing and gone to the adjoining dressing room, there was a long crimson robe laid out for her—one of Gayla's old gowns, Kendra assumed, too small for the Teenling. It fit Kendra perfectly; she dressed quickly and wandered back into the kitchen to find little Oki perched on a stool as

Gayla joyfully adorned each whisker with a tiny glitter ball. She had already used Eenberry paint to decorate his fur with large blue swirls.

It was Kendra's turn next. Gayla streaked her hair with red and green, painted her face with curly designs, and then set about braiding her hair with bobbles and bulbs.

"It's fantastic," Kendra beamed after Gayla had finished and stood her in front of the mirror.

"Come on," Gayla urged. "I don't want to miss anything."

"What about Unc—er, I mean your brother? Isn't he coming?" Kendra asked.

"Hmph!" Gayla replied as she ushered them out the door. "He's probably upstairs measuring his whiskers—as if the length of his beard will impress the elders! Don't worry about him; he'll show up in his own time."

The festival was held in a field on the banks of the River Wink, near the biggest Een town of Faun's End. During the short walk, Kendra couldn't help but dwell on the problem of the missing Kazah Stone, but such thoughts instantly evaporated as soon as her nose detected the first sugary smell from the fairgrounds. Soon the sounds of joyful cheers began to reach her ears, and the next thing she knew she was surrounded by crowds of costumed Eens. Here and there an Een would frolic past in a wide-hooped skirt or a bizarre crown-like cap. One old fellow was even wearing a tall stovepipe hat with a bird's nest on top! Inside the nest was a collection of purple eggs with green spots.

"Don't think of eggs!" Kendra joked, nudging Oki.

Before Oki had a chance to give a retort, they heard a loud squeal of delight. A flock of excited Eenlings roared past, chasing an enormous ball. This was a bauble ball, and if you have not heard of such a thing then it is perhaps best to describe it as a type of piñata, for it is made of colored paper and contains all sorts of trinkets, toys, and treats. Unlike a piñata, however, a bauble ball is cast with a bouncing spell so it has a life of its own, leaping here and there as it tries to escape the hordes of frantic Eenlings wanting to whack it with their toy wands. With each successful strike the ball lets out a loud bang—like a firecracker—until at last it bursts open to reveal its treasure trove of prizes.

"Come on," Gayla coaxed, skipping forward. "Let's play some games of our own."

The three of them were soon scampering through the grounds, trying their hand at every contest. These included many of Kendra's favorites, such as "Sneeze Race" (in which you wear wheel-skates and try to sneeze your way across a finish line), "Pickle Toss" (in which you throw a slippery pickle back and forth to your partner as many times as possible) and best of all, the "Boot Bang." In this one, you have to swing as high as you can on a swing and try to kick off your shoe, aiming for a long trumpet. If you actually succeed in getting your shoe down the trumpet, it spins down a long network of tubes, setting off a series of gears and gadgets until at last a melon ends up dropping—and exploding—on some hapless Een's head.

There were many other silly contests too, such as "Sink the Boat" (this involves cramming as many Eens as possible into a boat to see how many can fit in before it sinks), "Ticklefish" (in which you keep your feet in a tub full of Een fish as long as possible without breaking into laughter), and "Snore War" (a game to see who has the loudest snore—though it was usually impossible to award a winner, since everyone—including the judge—was asleep).

Kendra had the best day in a long while. She laughed until her face hurt, ate far too many sweets, and by early evening had that tired, happy, and slightly sick feeling one gets after spending the whole day at the carnival. They took a nap on the banks of the river, and when they awoke the meadow was just being cleared for dancing and more revelry. Many Eens were playing instruments—not only the narfoo, but the womboe, the fizzdiddle, and the flumpet, too.

Amidst this happy hullabaloo, the meadow soon filled with dancers young and old. Oki wandered off to find another

Eenberry cupcake, so Kendra amused herself by sitting on a toadstool next to Gayla, watching the dancers. Before long, a striking woman dressed all in white flashed in front of Kendra.

She looks familiar, Kendra thought, and then she realized it was none other than Winter Woodsong.

In her own time, Kendra knew Winter as an ancient woman, well over a hundred years old, for whom the slightest movement seemed to demand the most titanic effort. But now here she was thirty-five years younger and spinning across the meadow lawn as light as a cloud, her long braids waving like streamers in the light of the sinking sun. Kendra was amazed to see her move so sprightly.

The old woman caught Kendra staring and frolicked in her direction. "What now, young sorceress?" she inquired, pausing just in front of Kendra and Gayla. "Have you never seen an old woman dance?"

"You're not old," Kendra said—and she meant it. "You dance beautifully, Mistress Woodsong."

"Suck-up," Gayla muttered.

Winter looked at Gayla. "Now here is a face that would turn an Unger pale. Why so dour, my dear? Did you eat one of Luna Lightfoot's pucker-pears?"

Gayla glowered, and Kendra couldn't help wondering what had changed her mood. Then she noticed Gayla gazing over Winter's shoulder, across the field at a Teenling boy. He was dressed in a bright Jamboreen costume, but this was hardly as bright as his shock of red hair. Even from a distance, Kendra could see that the boy's eyes sparkled with kindness. Her heart took a little leap; for she knew at once that this was Krimson Kandlestar, the man who would one day become her father.

Winter Woodsong, it seemed, had known all along where Gayla was focusing her attention. She didn't even bother to turn around, but instead chuckled and said, "I am sure young Kandlestar would be most pleased to dance with you."

"Dance?" Gayla said brusquely. "With that twiddleberry?"

Then another Een girl sauntered past Krimson, flicking her long blonde hair and giving him a coquettish wave.

"Ugh," said Gayla with a derisive snort. "That Miranda Marigold is such a flirt; I ought to sock her."

"Now, now. Take heart," Winter chuckled. "There is more than one way to stir the soup."

With that, the impish woman grabbed Gayla and Kendra by the hands and whirled across the lawn, gamboling past the other dancers until they arrived right where Krimson was standing. Kendra watched in amusement as Winter twirled Gayla right into Krimson's arms—unfortunately, the boy

wasn't expecting it. He fell backwards with Gayla lying on top of him in a heap.

"Er . . . I'm sorry, Miss Griffinskitch," Kendra heard Krimson mumble awkwardly. His face had turned the same color as his hair—bright red.

"What's wrong with you?" Gayla snarled. "Aren't you going to ask me to dance?"

Krimson seemed at a loss for words, but he pulled himself to his feet, bowed slightly to Winter Woodsong, and whisked Gayla, who was still scowling, into the crowd of dancers.

"She sure is mean to him," Kendra murmured to Winter.

"Indeed," the old woman said. "Love is a cruel master."

Kendra wasn't sure what Winter meant by these words; but that was the sorceress for you. She always spoke in riddles.

Winter took Kendra's hand again, and together they frisked across the fairgrounds until they arrived at a small circular stage that had been erected near the riverbank.

"Ah, the Magicians' Match shall start soon," Winter declared. "I am the master of ceremonies, you know—so I suppose I now must take my leave. Perhaps I shall see you in the future, young sorceress." She gave Kendra a cryptic smile and then, in a wink, was off.

Kendra gave her braid a tug and turned to see Oki scampering forward.

"Did you see who's competing in the match?" the little mouse asked excitedly. "Look!"

He pointed up to the stage, where a few of the wizards were taking their places. One of them was a large gray raccoon. Kendra had to rub her eyes; why, for a moment she thought it was Ratchet! Then it occurred to her that not only was this raccoon thinner than her old friend, but he was also wearing a wizard's cape and holding a staff.

"I know what you're thinking," Oki told Kendra. "It's not Ratchet, though. It's his gramps, Roompa Ringtail! He's the one who designed our cloud ship. We built it based on his blueprints."

"I always wondered why it flew without any hiccups," Kendra remarked.

"I know," Oki said. "But old Roompa knew what he was do—EEK!"

Kendra didn't need to ask Oki what was wrong, for just then a hunched and growling Een strutted onto the platform. He looked a lot younger than the irascible Een Kendra knew from her own time, but there was no mistaking him: it was Burdock Brown, the wicked wizard who would one day crown himself the self-proclaimed Emperor of Een.

"*Poopensnautch*," Oki squealed nervously. "We're in trouble now!"

CHAPTER 11

A Muddle at the Magicians' Match

You've probably heard the expression, "Some people never change." This was certainly true of Burdock Brown, for all it took was one glance at the mean-spirited wizard for Kendra to realize that while he looked remarkably younger, he looked no less terrible. He scoffed and snarled, giving hint of the cruel tyrant he would one day become.

"Oh, don't think of eggs! Don't think of eggs!" Oki whimpered.

"Hush," Kendra said gently, trying to calm her own nerves at the sight of Burdock. "Remember, we're not his enemies here, not in this time. He doesn't even know who we are."

"Not yet, anyway," Oki squeaked.

"What's up with the furry fretter?" came a voice, and Kendra turned to see Gayla approaching.

"Oh . . . just the usual," Kendra replied, tugging on a braid. "Er . . . I thought you were dancing with Krimson."

"That pea-planting puddlehead?" Gayla growled, crossing her arms. "I punched him in the eye."

"Why!?" Kendra cried.

"He said I looked beautiful," Gayla explained. "What a jerk."

Kendra stared at the Teenling in bewilderment. "It sounds like a *nice* thing to say, if you ask me."

"Come on," Gayla said. "Let's just watch the match. I sure hope Burdock doesn't win."

"Me neither," Oki piped up.

The sun was now setting and Eens were streaming in from every corner of the fairgrounds to watch the Magicians' Match. Before long, the first stars began to appear in the sky and Winter Woodsong glided onto the stage.

"I'm afraid we have a slight dilemma," she said after a short introduction. "As you know, the Magicians' Match is always among seven—no more, no less. And yet we are down to six, for Master Thistledown has taken ill. Too many pucker-pears, it seems."

A light chuckle arose from the audience. After a moment, Winter continued. "What magic-maker amongst you will join the match?"

"Maybe Uncle Griffinskitch can enter," Kendra whispered.

"I keep telling you, Braids," Gayla said. "He's my brother, not my uncle. And besides, they stopped letting him compete after he won seven times in a row."

"Well, why don't *you* compete?" Oki asked.

"You know what, Eeks? That's the best idea I've heard all day." And with that Gayla marched towards the platform.

"Oh, dear," Oki murmured. "What a *mooflehead* I am! What if this changes the timeline? EEK! If we all turn into eggs it's going to be my fault!"

"No one's turning into eggs," Kendra insisted. "Let's just watch."

And watch they did, as Gayla strutted right up to the stage, brandishing her wand with a theatrical twirl. "I, Gayla Griffinskitch, shall compete in the Magicians' Match."

"You?" Burdock asked, his one eyebrow twitching. "You may be talented and beautiful, young apprentice, but you are not a wizard yet."

"Hmph," Gayla grunted. "Maybe you're just worried you'll lose."

Kendra watched Burdock's face burn red, though she couldn't tell whether it was from embarrassment or rage. Whatever emotion was percolating inside his decrepit heart, the nasty Een seemed to find a way to contain it, for he eventually said, "I'm not worried at all, my dear. Not at all. But we wouldn't want to make a mockery of the Match . . . would we?"

Kendra pulled furiously on one braid; it looked as if Gayla wanted to punch Burdock. Or worse. But just then Winter Woodsong stepped between them and proclaimed in a loud voice: "At times such as these we must remember the words of old Leemus Longbraids, founder of Een: 'Jamboreen is for one and all, the short and the tall.' So I shall let young Griffinskitch compete!"

Burdock gnashed his teeth. The audience cheered. It was highly unusual to have someone so young compete in the Match, and Kendra could instantly tell that Gayla had become a crowd favorite. The tempestuous Teenling raised her chin and proudly took her place at the end of the line alongside Roompa Ringtail, who offered her a smile of encouragement.

Then Kendra heard a humph and she turned to see her uncle standing next to her. She knew that type of humph. It was one filled with pride.

"It is always good to have a Griffinskitch in the game," he declared, though whether it was to her or no one in particular, Kendra wasn't sure.

Winter Woodsong now quieted the crowd with the lift of her pale hand and announced, "Let me remind you of the rules. This is a contest of pure Een wizardry. No potions, elixirs, or other enchanted items may be used—only the magic you can muster from yourselves and your wands. There shall be seven rounds. After each round, the elders"—here, Winter gestured to the side of the stage where some ancient Eens sat in a row—"shall confer, and the magician they deem has the least impressive trick shall be expelled, until at last we are left with our winner. Good luck to you all . . . and now, let the Match begin."

The first contest was called the Twilight Twirl. Here, each Een wizard would call forth an element of nature and command it to perform upon the stage. Perla Proudfoot went first; she summoned a cloud of flower petals that arched into the audience like a beautiful rainbow. Roompa went next and brought a flurry of snowflakes that whirled in the shape of two dancing fauns. It brought him much applause, and Kendra was almost sorry that Gayla had to follow him. But she performed well enough, singing with her strong mellifluous voice to command a cloud of white dandelion fluff to flutter in the whimsical shape of a winged horse.

"Humph," Uncle Griffinskitch muttered to Kendra and Oki. "She will win the hearts of Eens with that voice; but it will hardly help her if she ever finds herself face to face with an Unger."

After Gayla came Maybelle Moonbeam, Hektor Hootall, Dreydon Doon, and at last Burdock. He summoned a swarm of Een bees from the crowd—this was a particularly complicated feat, Kendra knew, to command a living, thinking being, and the bees were hardly pleased about it. But it seemed to Kendra that the judges thought it was all in good fun. They quickly conferred to make their decision, and after the first round Dreydon Doon was asked to leave the stage. Kendra and Oki cheered—Gayla had passed!

The next round was Flower Fancy, in which each wizard was asked to conjure a magical plant from a large pot of soil. This time, Maybelle Moonbeam went first; her plant blossomed with flowers that exuded the scent of Eenberry Pie. Hektor Hootall summoned a plant that grew strange and wondrous fruits. Perla Proudfoot's plant glimmered with light as bright as stars. Burdock Brown went fourth; he grew a thorn bush that snapped like a dragon and sent more than one Een scampering away (Oki would have fled too, but Kendra held his paw).

Then it was Gayla's turn. As Kendra watched while toying nervously with her braids, Gayla stood in front of her pot, waved her wand, and with a chant conjured a beautiful flower with glowing, luminescent bells. It spun towards the moon, blasting out beautiful music until at last . . .

It withered and died.

Gayla sighed in dismay, and lowered her wand in defeat as she stared at the brown and desiccated leaves that now drooped before her.

"Humph," Uncle Griffinskitch muttered. "She went too quickly."

Kendra opened her mouth to defend her mother, but one look at Uncle Griffinskitch made her change her mind. Instead, she focused her attention on the stage where Roompa was now ready to take his turn. The raccoon smiled at Gayla, told her she had given it a noble try, and then began to call and cajole, until from his pot there bloomed a strange and enchanting plant. It had bright red flowers and burst forth with tiny toys and trinkets that sent the Eenlings in the crowd squealing with delight.

It was no surprise to anyone that Gayla was expelled at the end of the round. Still, she held her head high as she left the stage.

"Pretty good, eh, Beards?" Gayla asked as she rejoined the audience. "I'm the youngest ever to make it past the first round."

"Aye," Uncle Griffinskitch snorted. "But you might have gone further."

"I thought you were sensational," Kendra told Gayla, but all she received in reply was a scowl.

On the contest went. With each round, another magician was ejected. Roompa was clearly winning over the crowd—especially during the Shadow's Duel. Here, the rascally raccoon coaxed his silhouette to tiptoe across the stage and, with much theatrics, kick Burdock's shadow right in the rear, so hard that it went flying from the stage. Burdock had to go collect it while the audience roared in laughter.

"Burdock doesn't look very happy," Kendra said.

"That's because Roompa's beating him at every turn," Gayla said. She looked over her shoulder to make sure her brother wasn't listening, then leaned closer and whispered, "If you ask me, Burdock tried to cheat."

"What do you mean?" Kendra asked in surprise.

"When I was up on stage I saw old Brownie sprinkle something on Roompa's wand," Gayla said. "Everyone else was watching Perla Proudfoot perform."

"That's not fair!" Oki squealed. "We have to tell someone!"

"Just calm down, Eeks," Gayla said. "Whatever Burdock did, it hasn't seemed to affect Roompa's magic yet. I just wished I knew what he was up to."

The final round was the Symphony of Stars, and to no one's surprise, the last two contestants were Burdock and Roompa. Burdock went first, chanting and waving his wand with great swagger. He lifted his arms to the air and gradually the stars began to sparkle and hiss, flaring to brightness as if they were tiny candles that had suddenly been transformed into bonfires.

Soon the whole sky was booming with a thunderous and threatening shower of stars. Streaks of light fired down towards the fairgrounds, causing many of the Eens to duck or run for cover. It was an impressive display to be sure, but Burdock could not sustain it for very long. After just a few seconds, his fireworks came to an end.

Roompa now took his turn. He strode to center stage, closed his eyes, and began to murmur. At first Kendra wondered if he had simply run out of magic, but then Oki tugged her sleeve and she looked up to see the stars begin to twinkle in the sky. At first Kendra didn't understand what was happening—then, suddenly she realized that Roompa was painting a picture with the stars, a wonderful constellation in the shape of the founder of Een, Leemus Longbraids. In one hand, the ancient wizard was holding his wand, and from it gushed a fountain of shooting stars.

"Wow," Kendra murmured. "It's beautiful."

"There's no doubt he's won!" Oki squealed in delight.

The crowd was cheering, but quieted as soon as Burdock strutted to the front of the stage, a nasty snarl smeared across his face. He snatched Roompa's wand from his paw and glared at it suspiciously "Wait a minute!? What is this?" Burdock demanded.

"You have some complaint to make, Master Burdock?" Winter Woodsong asked, flitting across the platform.

"Yes!" Burdock growled, angrily shaking Roompa's wand. "I do indeed. This crooked critter—Roompa Ringtail—is a cheater!"

CHAPTER 12

The Portal Behind the Portrait

It was one of those moments that sent the crowd into a stir. You know the type of moment, like when your principal suddenly makes a surprise announcement during assembly and everyone begins to whisper and murmur all at once. And Burdock loved it. This Kendra knew just from watching him strut across the platform, his chest puffing with importance. Roompa, on the other hand, looked completely flustered—*Just like Ratchet,* Kendra thought.

"Master Burdock," Winter Woodsong said, "this is a most serious accusation."

"I speak the truth," the arrogant wizard hissed, passing Roompa's wand to her. "Look, his Eenwood is covered with a powdery residue. And we all know Roompa experiments with all sorts of ridiculous potions and powders. I suspect he's tried to magnify the magic of his wand."

"Hmm," Winter murmured.

Kendra looked over at Burdock. He looked so pleased with himself that she wanted to kick him in the shin or zap him with her wand—anything to wipe that smug expression from his face. But it was Gayla who took action. In the beat of an Een's heart she was up on stage, confronting Winter Woodsong.

"No!" the girl blurted. "Don't listen to him! Burdock is the one who cheated!"

"What!?" Burdock growled, his one eyebrow twitching. "My dear, you're just upset because you lost."

Gayla whirled around and glared at him, a look that could stop a giant in its tracks. "I am *not* your dear," she snapped.

The frenzied conversation from the crowd grew louder; Winter had to bang her staff against the stage to gain attention.

"Young Griffinskitch," she said. "It is a serious affair to accuse a wizard of Een."

"But Brownie's accusing Master Ringtail," Gayla protested.

"That is Master Burdock to you," Winter declared. "And he is an equal of Master Ringtail."

"A wrong is a wrong," Gayla said. "No matter *who* commits it."

"Indeed," Winter said (though not unkindly, in Kendra's opinion). "So we shall let the elders decide this matter, in the privacy of the Elder Stone."

"No!" Gayla exclaimed, grasping Winter's wrist. "I'm telling you, Roompa won fair and square. Burdock is the liar and cheat!"

"ENOUGH!"

It was Uncle Griffinskitch. All this time Kendra had been tugging furiously on her braids, her eyes locked on Gayla, but

now she turned to see her uncle bustling through the crowd. His ears were burning red with rage.

"Eek!" Oki squealed, tightly clutching Kendra's sleeve. "This is all my fault! Oh, why did I tell Gayla to join the match?"

Uncle Griffinskitch quickly took to the platform and Kendra suddenly realized just how strong and imposing he looked. He hadn't bothered to costume himself at all for Jamboreen, and his dark grey beard and somber clothes stood in strong contrast to the colors that filled the stage.

"Gayla!" he growled.

But the Teenling girl paid him no mind. "Listen," she pleaded, still clinging to Winter Woodsong. "I'm telling you the truth."

"Humph," Uncle Griffinskitch grunted, grabbing Gayla by the shoulder and pulling her away. "Forgive my sister, Mistress Woodsong. She knows not her place."

"If it's to keep my mouth shut when I see someone doing wrong, then I know it well enough!" Gayla retorted, wrenching free of his grasp.

Uncle Griffinskitch glared down at her, his nostrils flaring. "You will apologize to Master Burdock."

Gayla looked at her brother with an expression of horror painted on her face. Even from afar, Kendra could read the message in Gayla's eyes. It said: *Please don't make me do this.*

But Uncle Griffinskitch was not about to be defied. Something passed between them. At last, after a long tense moment, Gayla hung her head in defeat.

"I-I'm sorry, Master Burdock," she blurted—then before another word could be said, she turned and fled from the stage, tears spilling down her cheeks.

"I'm going after her," Kendra told Oki. She lifted her robe to dart through the crowd—but she only made it two steps before a firm hand pulled her to a halt. She looked over her shoulder. Quick as a lightning bolt, Uncle Griffinskitch had managed to catch her.

"Let her go," he said.

"She's upset!" Kendra protested.

"Aye," Uncle Griffinskitch grunted sadly. "Aren't we all?"

Kendra cast a helpless glance in Oki's direction. "*Shuckleberries,*" he murmured in response. "I guess this Jamboreen is over."

Kendra and Oki slept in a proper bed that night—but not for long. Uncle Griffinskitch had them up at the crack of dawn, only a few hours after they had gone to sleep.

"If you're going to stay in my house, you can earn your keep," the ornery wizard grunted, as he finished the last of his dandelion tea. "The mousling can accompany me today when I go to the Elder Stone; I must attend the trial of Master Ringtail and I may need someone to run messages for me. Can you do that, mousling?"

Kendra knew that the last thing Oki wanted to do was spend the day with Uncle Griffinskitch, but the little mouse managed to squeak, "Y-yes, sir."

"As for you," Uncle Griffinskitch said, turning his steely gaze to Kendra, "you can clean the house."

"What about Gayla?" Kendra asked.

"Humph," the wizard grunted in an anxious, worried type of way. "She didn't come home." Then he looked sternly at Kendra. "Do you know where she is?"

Kendra shook her head, nervously twisting her braids.

"She must go before the elders and formally explain her accusation against Master Brown," Uncle Griffinskitch said. "If she returns home, tell her to go to the Elder Stone immediately. May the ancients help her if she does not!"

Kendra nodded and Uncle Griffinskitch shunted Oki out the door, leaving her all alone in the kitchen. Only a day ago, Gayla had been dancing across the floor, singing merrily, but now the house felt cold and somber, quiet as a tomb.

Kendra sighed and began tidying up the kitchen, her mind fretting. It only took her an hour to clean up the bottom part of the house; then she began scrubbing the long staircase that led to the upper chambers.

She had made it only halfway up when she suddenly noticed that one of the paintings on the wall was askew. It was an enormous portrait of an ancient Een wizard (Kendra couldn't remember who he was, just that he was some long-dead ancestor). Kendra had always disliked the picture, but now, as she reached for the heavy wood frame, she realized that it wasn't crooked at all. It just looked that way because

it was angled towards her, like a door that had been slightly ajar.

Strange, Kendra thought as she wriggled her fingers behind the frame. She tugged, and sure enough, the painting swung towards her, creaking ever so quietly on a pair of hidden hinges.

It *was* a door.

A strange mixture of scents reached Kendra's nostrils: dust, incense, and decaying parchment. Kendra instantly knew she had found an entry to her uncle's study. It was a private place, one that the old wizard kept hidden with secret doors and passageways. Kendra had managed to find her way in a few times as a child, but Uncle Griffinskitch was careful to relocate the door every few months. This particular portrait was an entryway that Kendra had never discovered before.

Why would he leave it open? she wondered. *It's not like Uncle Griffinskitch to be so careless.*

She couldn't resist the temptation to enter. Casting a wary glance over her shoulder, she tiptoed inside.

A long, narrow staircase spiraled up towards the top of the tree. Kendra began the climb, carefully feeling her way in the darkness. With each step the smells grew stronger, but it took a few minutes for her to reach the chamber itself. It was a gloomy place, utterly quiet. Row upon row of bookshelves towered over her head. More books could be found on desks and ledges, arranged in high piles. Here too were scrolls, parchments, and even a tusked skull. *An Unger,* Kendra thought with a shudder.

Suddenly she heard a noise, like the flip of a page, and it caused her to gasp—though she managed to catch the sound in her throat. Someone was in the room.

Kendra slowly turned and peered around one of the bookshelves.

It was Gayla.

She was sitting at a tall desk where an enormous book lay open before her, and she was reading it quietly to herself, tracing the lines of text with one long finger. She seemed completely lost in her own world, and for a moment Kendra just watched her. Then Gayla reached into her robe and lifted something to the faint light.

Kendra cried out in surprise. Gayla looked up, wide-eyed and startled; in her hand, brooding dark and purple, was the Kazah Stone.

CHAPTER 13
The Danger of a Lie

The Eens have a famous saying: "The sharpest burr is the one you find in your shoe," meaning that it's those closest to us who can cause us the most pain. Kendra had never really understood that adage until now. Why, she had been betrayed by her own mother—and it wounded her as surely as the slap of a dragon's tail.

"You lied," Kendra uttered as she stared at the wild Teenling girl. "You said you didn't steal my ring. But you did."

"It's not your ring," Gayla said defensively. "It's your master's."

"It *is* my ring," Kendra retorted. "He gave it to me."

"Why would a wizard entrust his twelve-year-old apprentice with a Kazah crystal?" Gayla demanded. "That's right, Braids; I know this is no ordinary rock."

"So?" Kendra snapped. "You still took it. You still lied."

Gayla gave her a dismissive wave and turned back to the mysterious tome that lay before her. "Look," she said. "It's all explained here. Kazah Stones come from the Kazah Caves in the Crystal Peaks, beyond the borders of Een. Kazah Stones have powers—strange ones, it says. And when you become a true Een wizard you are given your own Stone to wear. But those aren't pure Kazah crystals, just cut gemstones with the slightest of powers." She paused and gazed upon the ring in her open palm. "But this Stone . . . this Stone is round . . . perfectly round. Or at least it was before it cracked."

She seemed mesmerized by the Kazah Stone, and now Kendra stepped forward impulsively to touch it. Gayla instantly pulled back, cradling the ring close to her chest.

"The elders, the wizards, they keep everything so secretive," she said, staring at Kendra. Her eyes were wild and exhausted, and Kendra suddenly realized that she hadn't slept all night. "Who do you think sees these books?" Gayla asked, pointing at the shelves. "No one! You can't find them in the library. Old Beards keeps this knowledge squirreled away in his own private study, so that no one can learn, no one can understand the mysteries of Een. The mystery of Kazah." Gayla glared at Kendra. "You know it, don't you?" she asked in an accusatory tone. "You understand Kazah! Does it work? Does it do what the book claims?"

Kendra shook her head in bewilderment. "I don't know how to use it," she said. It was the truth.

"It says Kazah can let you hear an echo of the past or catch a glimpse of the future," Gayla murmured, gazing down at the dark purple Stone. "You just have to concentrate your will, focus your mind on a particular time."

"Like meditating," Kendra pondered, remembering her training with Uncle Griffinskitch.

"If you can imagine a specific time vividly, then you should be able to catch a glimmer of it through the Kazah Stone," Gayla said. "But some ancient Eens believed that Kazah could do more than just gaze upon time. They believed it could be used to travel *through* it."

Kendra fumbled for something to say. Gayla was staring at her with one raised eyebrow, expecting a response.

In the end, Kendra decided to change the subject. "You're wanted at the Elder Stone. It's Roompa's trial. And you're supposed to be there."

Gayla's expression thawed. "They think I'm lying. They think I made up the story about Burdock sabotaging Roompa's wand."

"Did you?" Kendra asked, the words leaping from her lips before she could think better of them.

"Don't you dare take his side, Braids," Gayla said, thrusting a finger at Kendra. "He's a terrible . . . disgusting man. You have no idea."

"As a matter of fact, I do," Kendra said hotly. "But . . . but you lied about taking the ring."

"So you think I lied about this?"

Kendra stared at her. She didn't know what to think. For such is the danger of a lie; like poison, it can seep into friendship's every crack, contaminating even that which is pure and true. Kendra had no trouble believing that Burdock had lied and cheated. She just couldn't be sure that Gayla wasn't doing the same.

"Come with me, okay?" Gayla implored. "I need someone in my corner right now."

"Give me back my ring," Kendra said. "And I'll come."

"I will. I promise," Gayla said. "Right after the trial."

"Why not now?" Kendra asked.

"I . . . I just need it for the trial," Gayla replied.

"Why?"

"Well, it might bring me some luck," Gayla said. "And let's face it. If they've called me before the council, I'll need all the luck I can get."

The Elder Stone was one of Kendra's favorite places in all the Land of Een. She loved its rainbow fountains and the cryptic stone faces that peered from every nook and cranny, each one seemingly with a story to tell. Yet today, there was not a moment to be spared marveling at the Stone's wonders.

As soon as they reached the grand hall, Gayla was ushered inside by a stern-looking badger with a set of nasty claws and an even nastier pike. Kendra was allowed to go as far as the door to the council chambers and then made to wait in the corridor. She spent several anxious moments sitting alone, until the doors opened a crack and Oki darted out to join her.

"Your uncle has had me running all over Faun's End asking after Gayla," the mouse explained. "But now that she's arrived, I have to wait out here."

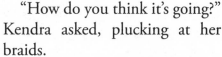

"How do you think it's going?" Kendra asked, plucking at her braids.

"Not well for Roompa," Oki replied. "Gayla's his only hope. But it sounds like she doesn't have a very good reputation. I guess she's been known to tell a fib or two."

"Tell me about it," Kendra sighed. "You were right; she's had the Kazah Stone the whole time."

"I'm sorry, Kendra," Oki said glumly. "I wish I had been wrong."

The trial didn't last long. Only an hour later, the doors to the council chambers opened and Roompa appeared, his head hung low in shame. He was quickly led away by the badger. Then Burdock strutted out, followed by Uncle Griffinskitch and a dejected Gayla.

"Looks like everything has been settled," Burdock declared, puffing out his chest. "Well, except for one last matter to arrange between the girl and me." He cast a salacious smile at Gayla. For a moment she looked as if she was forming some retort, but then she just flushed red, turned, and bolted down the corridor.

"Gayla—wait!" Uncle Griffinskitch called, but she was already gone.

"We'll fetch her," Kendra said, grabbing Oki's paw.

They headed off in pursuit of the temperamental Teenling and found her only a few moments later. She was sitting at the bottom of a lonely staircase, tears streaming down her face.

"They took away Roompa's wand," Gayla said. "*Permanently.* Can you believe it?"

"It's exactly what Ratchet said happened to his grandfather," Oki murmured thoughtfully. "He went to live in the southern outskirts of Een in shame."

"Who's Ratchet?" Gayla asked.

"Er . . . just a friend of ours," Kendra said. "But what about *you*? What did the council say?"

"I'm being punished too," Gayla said, wiping her cheeks with one sleeve. "They're going to suspend my training. They say I'm too arrogant. Too brash."

Kendra gasped. She couldn't help thinking that this wasn't the way things were supposed to turn out. How could her mother grow into one of Een's greatest sorceresses if she wasn't allowed to study magic?

Then Gayla reached inside her robe and pulled out the Kazah Stone. She cradled it in her palm, staring at it longingly. "I didn't lie," she said. "How come no one believes me?

Burdock's the one. He's getting away with it just because I'm so young and he's . . . he's so old."

Kendra looked down at Oki and sighed. She knew all too well the nature of Burdock's slippery tongue. He could charm a dragon from its egg.

"I can't stay here," Gayla whispered. "I need to be free. This place . . . it's like I'm being strangled. I can't live the life they're laying out for me."

"What are you talking about?" Kendra asked. "What life?"

"Don't you get it?" Gayla said in exasperation. "Burdock wants to marry me."

"That's disgusting!" Oki cried.

"And what about Krimson?!" Kendra exclaimed.

"He's just a gardener," Gayla said. "Beards wants me to marry someone 'proper.' Like a wizard. Like Burdock."

"But he wouldn't make you marry Burdock," Kendra persisted.

Gayla looked at her, wild-eyed. "This isn't a fairy tale, Braids. It's real life."

"But—,"

Gayla didn't let her finish. "I know you don't come from here," she said. "I worked it out. You come from the future, don't you? You *are* related to Krimson. You're his daughter or granddaughter or something aren't you? He went off and married some pretty girl, like that wretched Miranda."

Kendra pulled fiercely on her braids. She didn't know what to say.

"You have to get me out of here," Gayla urged. "You have to take me to your time."

"I-I can't," Kendra said. "I don't know how. We came by accident."

"Fine," Gayla said. "I don't need your help. I can do it without you." And with that she closed her eyes and clutched the Kazah Stone tight to her chest.

"What are you doing?!" Oki squealed.

"Shut it, Eeks, or I'll tie your tail in knot," Gayla snarled.

Then she breathed deeply, her whole body seeming to relax. Kendra could see she was disappearing into a quiet corner of her mind.

She's way better at meditating than me, Kendra thought. She could almost sense the world Gayla was imagining. It was another place, another time—one without Burdock.

Then the Kazah Stone began to glow. The whole corridor filled with a soft purple light that soon began to grow whiter and hotter.

"She's disappearing!" Kendra cried. She grabbed Oki's paw and clutched hold of Gayla's sleeve.

"Eek!" Oki squealed. "What about the timeline?"

It was too late. A sheet of white flashed in front of Kendra's eyes—then, in an instant, she felt herself sucked away.

CHAPTER 14

A Council of Strange Elders

If you have ever been stuck in a car or on a plane for more than a few hours, you've probably found yourself asking, "Are we there yet?" If only you had the Kazah Stone! By its magic you would reach your destination quicker than an Eenling's heartbeat. This was certainly the case with Kendra. One moment she had been blinded by the white light and the next everything had returned to normal. In fact, it felt *too* normal. Kendra was still with her friends at the bottom of the staircase in the Elder Stone, as if nothing had happened.

"I don't think it worked," Oki squeaked nervously.

"Of course it did," Gayla said. "Can't you sense it? The temperature is different. The smell, too. The Kazah Stone will drop you in the exact same physical place where you start from—it's just the *time* that's different."

"Oh," Kendra murmured, sniffing at the air. "That's why we were falling when we first used the Stone, Oki. When we went back in time the cloud ship didn't even exist yet—so we just started tumbling through the sky!"

"*Fuzzlewinkle,*" Oki murmured, clutching his forehead. "We have to be careful!"

"Don't be such a furry-worry, Eeks," Gayla chastised. "C'mon, let's go explore."

"Wait a minute," Kendra said. "You promised to give back the ring."

Gayla turned and looked at Kendra pensively. "Sure," she said, dropping the ring into Kendra's palm. "All I ever wanted to do was to escape. And now I have."

"But what time exactly have we escaped to?" Oki wondered. "When are we?"

"There's only one way to find out," Gayla declared, marching down the passageway.

Kendra and Oki exchanged a weary look and followed after the impetuous girl. They hadn't gone very far when they rounded a corner and found themselves before a larger-than-life statue of an old Een wizard.

"Oh, dear," Oki murmured.

"It's just stone, Freak Eek," Gayla said.

"I know that—but it wasn't here before," Oki said.

"Hmph," Gayla mused, casting a critical eye upon the statue. "Who is this old geezer, anyway?"

"He's Leemus Longbraids, one of the first elders of Een," Oki said. "Surely—,"

"BOR-ing," Gayla muttered. "C'mon; let's keep moving."

She continued down the passageway with Oki shaking his head after her. Kendra couldn't help but linger and gaze upon the statue, with its long, tangled beard and solemn expression. Then she noticed an inscription at the base of the statue: *Fret not the future, nor pine for the past.*

Kendra plucked at a braid, only to realize her friends were no longer in sight. She hurried to catch up, pondering the inscription.

It wasn't long before they neared the council chambers. They could hear footsteps—a lot of them—so Gayla slowed everyone down and together they cautiously peered around a corner of the passageway.

They had arrived at the palatial doors to the council chambers, and here a number of Eens were headed inside. Kendra counted five elders. Two were old Eens, but the rest were all Een animals: a hedgehog, a toad, and an owl.

"This is odd," Kendra whispered. "In the time Oki and I come from Een animals aren't even allowed in the Elder Stone, let alone allowed to be elders."

"Really?" Gayla snorted. "If we're not in your time, then just when have we landed?"

A sixth elder now came into view. This was an incredibly ancient woman and she instantly captured Kendra's curiosity. She was leaning heavily on a twisted stick of Eenwood, so there was no doubt that the woman was an old and powerful sorceress. But there was something that seemed to ail her, something more than old age. Kendra couldn't quite put her finger on it.

Then the old sorceress turned and stared right at the corner of the passageway where they were hiding. Kendra instinctively shrank back, but noticed that the woman's eyes were wide and vacant, as if she was staring not at Kendra, but *through* her.

"She's blind," Gayla murmured.

The ancient woman put one crooked finger to her lips, as if to make a "shhh" sound. Kendra gave her head a shake. Had she really seen that? The old sorceress merely smiled, then turned her head and hobbled into the council chamber. A tiny ladybug came last (he held a spear, so he was clearly the Captain of the Een Guard) and shut the doors behind him.

"We have to listen in on their meeting," Kendra announced.

"Eek! Why?" Oki squealed.

"There's something strange about that old woman," Kendra said. "I think I know her. Besides, it wouldn't be the first time we spied on a meeting."

"I know," Oki said. "And the last time we did, we were forced to go on a long, dangerous quest chasing dragons and Ungers, and—don't forget—I was turned into an onion."

"You were turned into an onion?" Gayla asked. "Well, now we have to spy."

"Why?" Oki asked.

"Because, Eeks," Gayla said. "I want to see what happens to you next."

It took a bit more urging, but eventually Oki led them back down the passageway and through a series of corridors. He had once worked as a messenger mouse for the elders, so he guided them with confidence until at last they arrived before a plain wooden door.

"Well, here we go again," he squeaked.

They crept through the door and found themselves in a tiny alcove. At one end was a thick red curtain; it was the only thing separating them from the meeting chamber.

"Be very quiet," Oki warned in a whisper.

Gayla sneered at the little mouse, but held her tongue. All three of them poked their noses through the curtain and gazed upon the chamber. It was small and rather dimly lit, with seven chairs positioned around a small pool. All the chairs were now filled—save one.

Then the ladybug stepped forward and announced, "Make way for the Eldest of the Elders."

A small door in the far corner of the room opened, and there appeared a tiny, grizzled creature. It was so bent and frail, its fur so patched and white, that it took a moment for Kendra to recognize it as a mouse. With strenuous labor, the feeble creature shuffled to the final remaining chair where a large trumpet-shaped horn was positioned.

"Fiddle all!" the mouse exclaimed as he put one ear to the horn. "Is this contraption working?"

"It works, old friend," the blind sorceress said.

"It burps?" the mouse asked. "Who's burping?"

"No one is burping," the sorceress replied. "I said it WORKS. Come closer to the horn."

"Let me help," the ladybug declared, skittering over to the trumpet and sliding it closer to the mouse.

"He's deaf as a stone," Gayla whispered from behind the curtain. "Quite a council we've got here. One of the elders can't see and one of them can't hear. This is going to be a long meeting."

"Fiddle all," the ancient mouse said. "That's better. We ought to call in the inventor of this hearing horn and have them make a few adjustments."

"In that case, old friend, call yourself," the blind sorceress remarked. "After all, the inventor of the hearing horn is *you.*"

"Ah, yes," the mouse responded. "How could I forget?"

"Because you're older than dirt," Gayla muttered from their hiding place.

"Shhh," Kendra hissed. "You'll get us caught."

But they escaped detection, and the ancient mouse now brought the meeting of the elders to order. "Welcome, friends," he greeted, his voice crackling with age. "We have assembled for a grave purpose: to hear the pleas of Shaden Shiverbone and to decide the future of his apprentice."

A murmur passed through the elders; Kendra could sense anxiety in the chamber. She scavenged her memory for the name Shaden Shiverbone, but she was sure she had never heard of him.

"Captain Ibb, call forth our wizard," the blind elder said.

The ladybug scurried over to the main chamber doors, swung them open, and escorted a pair of Eens into the circle. The older of the two was dressed in a dark robe and would have seemed quite imposing, if not for the worried expression upon his face. His head was bald, though he had thick side-burns and wild, untamed eyebrows.

"Look how long his staff is," Gayla whispered to Kendra and Oki. "He's not that old; he must be powerful to have such a wand."

The second Een, the apprentice, was a boy barely older than Kendra. He had a thick crop of luxurious, golden hair and he was dressed in a tunic of vivid turquoise, a color that matched his startling blue-green eyes. Kendra might have thought him handsome, but he strutted in a way that made him seem arrogant and spoiled. Then the boy turned his head so that Kendra could see him from a different angle, and she caught him curling his lip in a sneer that sent a sudden shiver down her braids. She had seen that sneer only once before— but there was no mistaking it.

"Days of Een!" she murmured. "That boy is Agent Lurk!"

CHAPTER 15

The Magic of Master Shiverbone

We've all had those moments in our lives when we've accidentally broken something precious and beautiful, like a vase or an ornament, and then tried in vain to repair it. For these delicate and fragile things, no amount of glue will ever return them to perfection. And every time we look at their cracks and chips, we will always remember how flawless they once looked.

This was the very sort of sinking feeling Kendra was now experiencing as she gazed upon Agent Lurk. She was looking at the face of a boy that seemed the shiny beacon of beautiful perfection, while at the same time knowing that it would one day be horribly maimed and disfigured. And it made her feel sick to her stomach.

Yet, if it made Kendra feel sick, she realized at once that it struck terror in Oki. He began to tremble and it was all Kendra and Gayla could do to clamp their hands over the little mouse's mouth in order to prevent him from bursting into a fit of eeking.

"Why is he so worried about that pretty boy?" Gayla asked Kendra in a hushed whisper.

"He's not pretty at all in our time," Kendra replied. "He's maimed and hideous. And he's been chasing us."

"Mmpheek!" Oki squealed beneath the layer of hands keeping him quiet.

"Shut your eek-hole, you furry fretter!" Gayla threatened. "We're going to let go of you now, and you're going to be quiet! Otherwise, I'll kick you into that chamber with Golden Boy there."

Oki's eyes grew large as two Eenberry pies and he nodded in understanding. Slowly, Kendra and Gayla let go of him, and they all turned their attention back to the scene in the chamber.

They had missed all the formal introductions and now caught Master Shiverbone in mid-sentence.

". . . So I ask for leniency," the wizard implored, wringing his hands nervously. "True, my apprentice has shown some error in judgment. But his abilities cannot be denied. I have seen him tame a skarm with a mere word."

"I, too, have watched this boy," spoke the hedgehog elder. "And he *is* powerful. But he is also arrogant. Such is not the way of an Een wizard; this much you should know, Master Shiverbone."

"Three times have you taken him before the ancient tree of Een," added the blind sorceress. "And three times he has been

denied a wand. The tree is wise, Master Shiverbone. In the magic of Een, we must trust."

"I can make something of him," Shaden Shiverbone declared in an impassioned burst. "I know it."

"Master Shiverbone, we do not question your devotion," the mouse, Eldest of the Elders, observed. "You have shown fathomless patience with the boy. Now it is time for him to embark on another path. One that does not involve magic."

From her hiding place, Kendra could see Leerlin Lurk turning red. He snarled and his eyes bugged from his face; it looked as if he was trying to swallow a sack of nails. At last the boy could contain his fury no longer. Pushing Master Shiverbone aside, he stepped in front of the Eldest of the Elders and boomed, "How dare you deny me!?"

It wasn't his rage that surprised Kendra—it was his voice. The Agent Lurk she knew spoke only in hisses, like a snake. But this boy's voice was as clear and pure as a bell. *Whatever injured him destroyed even his throat,* Kendra thought with a shudder.

"How dare you speak in such a tone!?" Captain Ibb growled at Agent Lurk. "This is the Eldest of the Elders that sits before you, one of the greatest Eens in all of history. If not for he and our Mistress,"—here, the bug gestured to the blind sorceress—"then who knows where we might be? They have led Een to its grandest triumph."

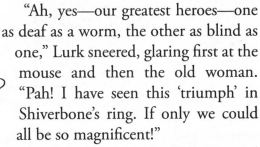

"Ah, yes—our greatest heroes—one as deaf as a worm, the other as blind as one," Lurk sneered, glaring first at the mouse and then the old woman. "Pah! I have seen this 'triumph' in Shiverbone's ring. If only we could all be so magnificent!"

And with that the boy turned and stormed from the chamber, slamming the great doors behind him with such a thunder that Shaden Shiverbone gasped and fell to one knee.

"What have I done?" he murmured, holding his forehead in one hand. "Forgive me, council. I believed in the boy. But his insolence has grown like a weed."

"Do not fret, Master Shiverbone," the old mouse said in a grave tone. "You are a gifted wizard, perhaps the most gifted Een has ever known. Why, you invented a cloak of shadows, to turn yourself invisible. And you have crafted the Kazah Stone, letting us gaze upon the past. You have etched your place in the books of Een history. And the boy shall find his, this I know all too well. I will have a word with my friend Choonta Chirpsong; perhaps she can find a place for him in the gardens of . . . "

But Kendra didn't hear the rest, for now she turned from the curtain and looked excitedly at Oki and Gayla. "Master Shiverbone made the Kazah Stone?" she wondered out loud. "That means Agent Lurk must have stolen it from him."

"What are you talking about?" Gayla asked. "I thought you got it from *your* master."

"I did," Kendra explained quietly. "But he got it from Lurk . . . but not this Lurk—the deformed one."

"But he's still the same age!" Oki squealed.

"Don't you see?" Kendra said in a hushed tone. "Lurk time-traveled; he must have. Days of Een! It's like one big puzzle. I wish I knew what time we're in now."

"Oh, *humdiggle*," Oki fretted. "Don't think of eggs! Don't think of eggs!"

"Give it a rest, Eeks," Gayla whispered, glancing back through the curtain. "Look, the council is ending."

Kendra peered back through the curtain and watched the chamber empty. Soon the only two Eens left were the blind sorceress and the ladybug. Kendra felt like the elder was staring at her again. She closed the curtain quickly and took a step back into the alcove.

"She's giving me the creeps," Kendra said. "Let's get out of here."

Gayla nodded. "For once, I'm going to agree."

But just as they turned to go, the thick red curtain was thrown open and there stood the ladybug, brandishing his spear. "Halt, in the name of Een!" he commanded.

"EEK!" Oki shrieked.

Kendra stared at the point of the ladybug's spear. She had no doubt that he had the strength and skill to use it. Then she heard a chuckle and looked up to see the old woman hobbling across the chamber, towards them. Blind though she might be, she navigated around the chairs and other would-be obstacles in the chamber with sureness of foot and soon stood right in front of Kendra.

"Thank you, Captain Ibb," the sorceress said with a nod at the ladybug. "You have performed your duty with admirable aplomb, as usual."

"We didn't do anything," Gayla told the elder.

"To the contrary, my dear," the blind sorceress tittered happily. "You have done a great many things, a great many things indeed."

She looked meaningfully at them with her empty eyes and Kendra couldn't help but be repulsed. There was nothing natural about those eyes. The irises were white, as if somehow they had been milked of all color, leaving only a ghostly, vacant stare.

It was enough to send Kendra shuffling behind Gayla, thinking to hide behind her. But the old sorceress reached out and grabbed Kendra by the hand. "Do not flee, child. I need to speak to you."

"M-me?" Kendra stammered. The elder's hand felt cold and frail. Kendra didn't dare wrench her hand away, worried that such sudden force might snap the old woman's fingers.

"Yes, you," the elder told Kendra. "Captain Ibb will entertain your friends for a moment or two."

She spoke a few quiet words to the ladybug and led Kendra across the floor of the council chamber, through a tiny door, and into a small and cozy room with a few odd paintings, a table stacked with books, and two stools. The old woman took a seat and gestured to Kendra to take the other. A pot of steaming tea awaited them, which the blind sorceress served without spilling a drop.

For the longest time the ancient woman sat with her tea, humming between each sip. Kendra tried to wait patiently, but at last could contain her curiosity no longer and exclaimed, "What do you want with me? Are we waiting for the Eldest of the Elders? Am I in trouble? I didn't mean to—,"

"Hush, child," the old woman said, firmly but kindly. "Not so quickly now; you'll give my head an ache. I forgot how impatient you are!"

"Oh," Kendra said. "Do I know you then?"

"Interesting question," the elder replied with a cryptic smile. "Do we ever truly know ourselves?"

Kendra tugged on a braid. The way the sorceress spoke reminded her of Winter Woodsong—she always seemed to answer a question with a question.

"Perhaps it is best to say that you do not know me," the old woman said eventually. "But I know *you*."

"How can that be?" Kendra asked.

"Because!" came the reply. "Have you not guessed it? I *am* you!"

CHAPTER 16

Kendra and the Sorceress of Sight

Kendra

dropped her tea-cup; it would have shattered against the floor, but the sorceress waved her staff and lifted the cup to safety. Kendra stared at the old woman, her mouth agape. "What do you mean?"

"I am you, one hundred years in the future," the ancient sorceress explained. "At least I am whom you might become if everything goes as I remember it."

You can certainly imagine Kendra's shock at this moment. She gazed at the sorceress in wonder, her mind a tumult of thoughts—and yet she knew, without doubt, that the old woman was telling her the truth. Somewhere, beneath all the cracks and wrinkles, Kendra could see her own face. Gayla had brought them to the future, one where she was old and hunched and . . .

"Blind," Kendra blurted out loud. "You're blind."

The elder Kendra laughed. "Just because I am blind doesn't mean I can't see," she said. "Didn't Uncle Griffinskitch teach us that?"

"He taught me to see with my mind, while I meditate," Kendra protested. "That's different from actually being blind!"

"Is it now?" the sorceress mused.

Kendra stared into the old woman's face—her own face—and felt lost in the maze of ancient wrinkles. *Will I ever really be that old?* she wondered. *Will I really go blind?*

"I know," the elder Kendra said, as if reading her thoughts. "It fiddles with the mind, doesn't it? I imagine this is all just a little overwhelming for you."

"Doesn't it hurt?" Kendra asked.

"What?" the sorceress asked.

"To . . . to be so old," Kendra stammered. "To be blind! Can't you just fix your eyes? You know, with magic?"

"I'm afraid there are some things that even magic cannot fix. But do not fret. I am like your Kazah Stone. My true power lies in my brokenness."

"But . . . but . . . I don't want to be blind!" Kendra exclaimed.

"And who says you will be?" the old woman asked, leaning forward on her staff, her voice suddenly becoming serious.

"Because you are," Kendra said. "This is my future."

"Humph," the sorceress grunted, sounding all too similar to Uncle Griffinskitch. "That is why I wished to speak with you, Kendra, to tell you about the fabric of time. Yes, this could be your future, but it is just one possibility. Any number of things can happen yet in your life, changing our path."

"That's what Oki always worries about," Kendra murmured—then a realization struck her and caused her to gasp. "Oki!" she exclaimed. "He's the . . . the . . . "

"Eldest of the Elders," the sorceress confirmed. "Do not be so surprised. Why, how many times has he saved us? And, besides, he is older than us—even if only by a little bit."

Kendra could suddenly hear Lurk's words in her mind, the ones he had spoken after they had captured him on the cloud ship: *'I would rather live in Burdock's kingdom than by the rules of your council.'* At the time Kendra had thought Lurk was speaking to her—but he wasn't, Kendra now realized. He had been speaking to Oki.

"Yes, in this future Oki leads the Council of Elders—with our help, of course," the elder Kendra said. "And all is well in the Land of Een. Well, for the most part. But it is not guaranteed that it will turn out this way."

"It could turn out better?" Kendra asked hopefully. She was still thinking about being blind.

"Or worse," the sorceress said gravely. "Many choices lie before you, Kendra. Even as we speak, Leerlin Lurk steals the shadow cloak and the Kazah Stone from Master Shiverbone's study. You must understand that the Stone is not cracked, not in this time. It is round and pure, without blemish or imperfection. But Leerlin will try to pry forth the power of the Stone, so that he might travel back through time. And he will succeed, Kendra, he will succeed—though at a terrible price."

"He's going to be maimed," Kendra murmured, shuddering even as she thought again of Agent Lurk's hideous face.

"Indeed," the sorceress said. "Kazah will rupture, and the crack will form. The crack is the key, child. When the Stone was perfect, one could merely gaze into the past or the future. But the crack means . . . "

"We can actually slip through time," Kendra said.

"Yes," the sorceress said. "Leerlin will use his foolish and unpracticed knowledge of dark magic to try and master the Kazah Stone—but it will crack in a terrible explosion, ripping him to shreds as it sucks him into its fissure. He will be hurtled into the past, and will awaken in the Land of Een, in the time of my childhood—your time—his body as bent and disfigured as his heart. He will still have the Stone, of course, but he will have no magic left to use it again. And so he will carry it as a mere token of his journey—until Uncle Griffinskitch takes it from him."

Kendra fidgeted with her braids; it normally helped her think, but right now her mind was in such a buzz that she knew all the braids in the world wouldn't be enough to clear her head. "Why?" she asked finally. "Why did Lurk want to travel back in time?"

"His heart throbs like a nest of skarm," the sorceress

replied. "He is furious that the council denies him the study of magic. So Leerlin will try to change the past. Once he finds himself in your time, he will ingratiate himself with Burdock Brown. They are like two thorns in the same paw; Burdock will make Leerlin his agent, and then that poor, misguided boy will do everything in his power to take away our greatest

triumph. He is on a mission of revenge."

"This is all so confusing," Kendra fretted. "What is the greatest triumph that everyone keeps talking about?"

"It is not a triumph yet—not for you anyway," the sorceress said. "That depends on the decisions you make, how you decide to use Kazah."

"Do you know what?" Kendra announced, abruptly rising to her feet. "I can go back in time myself. I can stop Lurk. I can stop Burdock from cheating in the Magicians' Match. I can find a way to make sure I don't lose my family. I can change *everything*."

For a moment the sorceress said nothing. Kendra stared at her and the ancient woman just returned the gaze with her wide and vacant eyes, as if she actually could see. It made Kendra shiver.

"Everything?" the sorceress said eventually. "Be careful, child. Start pulling at the tapestry of time, and everything you know may unravel. Remove a single thread, no matter how seemingly insignificant, from the timeline and everything you know— friends, family, even yourself—may change or cease to exist. But in your timeline everything has turned out well, so far."

"How can you say that!?" Kendra demanded. "Kiro's an Unger! I don't have a family! I want to find them! I want to find my mother!"

"It looks like you already have," the old sorceress said, nodding towards the door where, beyond, Gayla and Oki were waiting.

"You know what I mean," Kendra growled in frustration. "My proper mother. Who she should be in my time. I want to save her."

"Oh, Kendra," the old sorceress murmured. "What you

might worry about is saving yourself. You are so determined to control things. To make sure everything turns out a certain way. But how do you know all of this isn't happening as it should? Sometimes we have to learn to surrender."

"No," Kendra said. "We have to make decisions."

"Indeed," the sorceress said. "But you are too attached to the outcome of those decisions. Take action, send your intention into the universe—but be not so bold as to demand how that call should be answered."

"You don't make any sense."

The elder Kendra sighed. "I know it's hard for you. But I'm trying to help you. I'm trying to prevent you a mountain of pain. Why do you think I wanted to speak to you?"

"To make me crazy."

"No," the sorceress said with a gentle smile. "To help you. To talk about the Rumble Pit."

"The Rumble Pit!?" Kendra exclaimed. "What does that have to do with anything? It's in the past."

"What happened in that terrible gladiator arena is not yet solidified in the timeline," the sorceress explained cryptically. "Listen to me carefully, Kendra. There are choices ahead of you. If you do not make the right ones, then everything you know about your own time will be changed."

"And what does that mean?" Kendra asked, taking her seat again.

"It means," the old woman warned, "that those you know and love in your own time—the peryton, Trooogul, even Uncle Griffinskitch—will die."

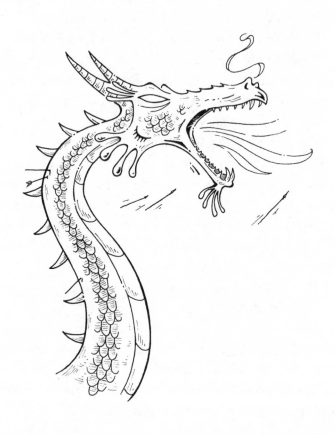

CHAPTER 17

The Power of the Cosmic Key

We've all received warnings in our lives. Normally they are about things that *could* happen if we don't behave in a certain way. Kendra instantly knew this warning was different. Just by contemplating the old woman's face, Kendra could tell that she spoke with a knowing wisdom, as if she had seen something in the past that was heart-wrenching and bleak. It showed in every fissure of her ancient face. It gleamed in her eyes, those giant windows that seemed to see nothing—and at the same time everything.

"D-die?" Kendra sputtered. "How? What's going to happen?"

The elder Kendra flashed a sad smile. "Tell me, child," she said after a moment, "what do you remember about the Rumble Pit?"

"You should know," Kendra grumbled impatiently. "If you're me, then it means you were there."

"Tell me anyway; I must know how it happened in *your* memory."

Kendra sighed. "I went there to save Trooogul—and I found him. But then we both ended up in the rumble." Here Kendra quivered, remembering the terrible clash of all the creatures that had been forced to fight in that pit of doom. Their screeches and roars still echoed in her memory.

"Please continue," the old sorceress urged.

Kendra nodded. "Well, Trooogul fought his way out of the pit, carrying me along with him. Then there was Queen Krake, that terrible lizard giantess. She had the Shard from Greeve at that point—but Trooogul fought her and took it. Then he fled."

"You didn't go after him?"

"You know I didn't!" Kendra cried in exasperation. "Some-how—I don't know how—the queen was gone. And then I heard my friend—our friend—the peryton, the winged deer. He was still in the pit, and he was horribly injured. So I let Trooogul go and went back into the pit to help the peryton. Then Uncle Griffinskitch came; he healed the peryton and we escaped in Ratchet's cloud ship."

"Hmmm," the sorceress murmured. "But Uncle Griffin-skitch and Ratchet were in Burdock's dungeon, all the way back in the Land of Een. How did they escape? How did they find out you were in the Rumble Pit?"

"I don't know," Kendra said. "I asked Uncle Griffinskitch—but he said I wouldn't believe him, even if he told me."

"And what does that mean to you?" the sorceress asked.

"I assumed he just used magic to escape," Kendra replied.

"Indeed," the sorceress said. "*Your* magic. Don't you see, child? You *do* need to go to the past. But not to the time you are thinking of. The one who rescues Uncle Griffinskitch from Burdock's dungeon is *you*."

"This doesn't make any sense!" Kendra exclaimed. "One minute you're telling me not to mess with the timeline; the next you say I have to."

"Am I?" the sorceress asked. "From my perspective, that event is in the past. It's exactly how I remember it happening. But if you don't rescue Uncle Griffinskitch, he won't go and rescue us from the Rumble Pit. There's more . . . much more. But that's all I can tell you. Rescuing Uncle Griffinskitch is the first step."

Kendra leaned back on her stool, feeling deflated. "You know all the answers already," Kendra told the old woman. "You know how it turns out. So just tell me! Tell me about our mother."

"You will have to take her with you," the sorceress said. "She has a part to play in all of this. There are things she must see."

"No, that's not what I meant," Kendra said. "I mean, do we ever find her again? In our time? What happened to her after she left the Land of Een and disappeared? You know, when I was a baby?"

"And if I answer those questions, what will that mean to you?" the sorceress asked.

"It will make me happy," Kendra said.

"Humph," the sorceress grunted. "That depends on the answers."

"It's unfair," Kendra said. "How do you know if you tell me that it won't all turn out the way it should?"

"Are you presuming that I know the way it should turn out?" the elder Kendra asked. "How do I know that even by meeting with you now, telling you to go rescue Uncle Griffinskitch, that it will turn out the way I remember it?"

Kendra rubbed her forehead and groaned. "Now, I'm the one with the headache," she complained. "You're talking in circles."

"I know," the sorceress said. "All of this talk of time travel; it makes the mind dance, wild and crazy, like a moth searching for the light. Listen, child. Do not think too hard. Just feel. That is the secret to the Kazah Stone."

"I know," Kendra said. "The Stone takes you to the time you're thinking about."

"Thinking is not enough," the sorceress emphasized. "You must connect your thought with *feeling*. It is the emotions that resonate with Kazah. A thought without feeling is like a bird without wings; it simply won't fly."

Kendra nodded and pestered a braid.

"The Kazah Stone is very powerful, of course—but its magic is not bottomless," the sorceress said. "You must be mindful of the crack. With each journey, it widens."

"What do you mean?" Kendra asked.

"Why, the Kazah Stone is like a cosmic key, taking you through all the doorways of time," the blind woman explained carefully. "But every jump strains it. You will only be able to use that ruptured Stone a certain number of times before it crumbles apart, its power forever exhausted."

"And then what will happen?" Kendra asked.

"You will be stuck forever in whatever time you are visiting," the elder Kendra said thoughtfully.

"How many jumps can we make then?" Kendra asked. "What should I do after I rescue Uncle Griffinskitch? Should I come back here? Should I stay in that time? What about Gayla? Don't I need to get her back to *her* time?"

"As I told you, there is something our mother must see," the sorceress said.

"What thing?" Kendra demanded. "What does it look like? What is she supposed to do?"

"Supposed to do?" the elder Kendra mused. "She will do what she must, I suppose! Kendra, relinquish control! I warn you as solemnly as I can: if you attempt to control the events of the past, to sculpt them to your own desire, it will lead to *disaster.*"

Kendra's mind was spinning again, like a whirlpool. "Listen," she said. "I need to know if—,"

"I am afraid our time is at an end," the elder Kendra interrupted. "There are no more answers I can give you. Trust your instincts, child; you will know what feels right."

"But—,"

"Shh," the old woman admonished, rising now from her seat and shuffling to the door. "Go now," she said. "Fetch your companions, and slip through the crack in Kazah. Our future, Kendra, is in your hands."

CHAPTER 18

In the Dungeons of the Elder Stone

As Kendra rejoined her friends in the ante-chamber, she couldn't help feeling like she had just finished a long and difficult day of school. You've probably had those types of days, filled with complicated math formulas and scientific equations. Even though you do your best to understand everything, all you end up with is a headache.

"What's going on, Braids?" Gayla asked, hand on one hip. "You look like you've been trampled by a pack of Orrids."

"This is no time for chitchat," Captain Ibb stated seriously. "I have been instructed to take you to the depths of the Elder Stone."

"EEK!" Oki squealed. "To the dungeons?"

"There are no dungeons in the Elder Stone," the serious ladybug replied. "Not anymore, at least. I have no idea why my mistress wishes you to go there, but those were her instructions and I do not question them."

With this said, Captain Ibb turned and marched out of the chamber.

Kendra moved to follow, but Gayla grabbed her by the wrist and jerked her back. "Just hold it, Braids," Gayla said. "I don't know about Eeks here, but I'm not going anywhere until you tell us what's going on."

Kendra grimaced. In her possession was a ring that could take her to any place, to any time, and yet here she was, stuck. What exactly was she supposed to tell Gayla? *Look, my hundred-and-twelve-year-old self just told me I have to go back in time and rescue my master—which happens to be your brother. And oh, by the way, you're my mother. And apparently there's something you have to see too, but who knows what?*

"Well?" Gayla asked, crossing her arms.

Kendra took a deep breath. "The sorceress, er . . . she just said I have to rescue my master from the old dungeons of the Elder Stone," Kendra said. "And we have to use Kazah to do it."

"We?" Gayla snorted. "Hmph. You want me to go back in time? I just escaped Burdock. I'm not going back home. Not now. Not ever."

"It's not your time we have to go to," Kendra said. "It's mine."

"But Kendra," Oki murmured, tugging on her sleeve. "How are we . . . I mean, what if . . . "

Kendra knew what he wanted to ask: *What's going to happen when Uncle Griffinskitch and Gayla come face to face with each other?* It wasn't a question Kendra could answer. But there was no use thinking about it anymore; it was time to do what the older sorceress said, and just trust.

"Please," she told Gayla. "I need your help."

"Fine," Gayla sneered after a moment. "But I'm only coming because you and Eeks are bound to make a colossal mess of things without me."

Just then, Captain Ibb reappeared in the chamber. "I thought I had made it clear that you were to follow me," he growled.

"We're coming," Kendra said, quickly falling in line behind the ladybug.

They were soon back in the complicated network of passageways that snaked through the Elder Stone. Captain Ibb led them ever downwards through a series of spiraling staircases and across stone bridges that spanned wide chasms. They were soon so deep that there

were no longer any windows; Captain Ibb lit a torch to guide their way.

"I never knew the Elder Stone went so deep," Oki murmured. "This is way farther down than I've ever been!"

When they finally came to a halt, Kendra could tell they were in a part of the Elder Stone that no one had been in for a long, long time—maybe decades. The air had a heavy, musty stench and a thick layer of dust covered the floor. Then Kendra noticed a row of dark, gaping holes on one side of the passageway: the abandoned dungeon cells. They looked like giant mouths, for the top and bottom of each opening was ridged with jagged stumps of wood—all that was left of the prison bars.

"I shall now take my leave," Captain Ibb announced abruptly. With a farewell nod, he turned and marched away with his torch, leaving them in complete darkness.

"Charming fellow," Gayla muttered. She took out her wand and with a quick flick of her fingers caused the top to glow, producing a faint illumination. "So here we are," she said. "What's your plan, Braids? What do we do once we reach the new time?"

"Er . . . I'm not really sure," Kendra said.

"Just going to make it up as we go along?" Gayla asked. "For once, I admire your style."

"Oh, dear," Oki murmured. "Maybe we should just come back tomorrow, once we've made a proper plan. And had a nice cup of tea. And—,"

"What else?" Gayla snarled. "A scrambled egg with toast? Just give it a rest, Eeks. Braids said we have to do this now—so let's hop to it."

Kendra nodded, fished the Kazah Stone from her robe, and placed it on her finger. "Here we go," she murmured.

She closed her eyes, and began to think of Uncle Griffin-skitch, locked away in the dungeon cells. The dungeon part wasn't hard to imagine—she could already feel the cold stones beneath her feet, taste the dust in the air. She just had to think of her uncle in this very spot, and get the timing right. It took her several minutes to quiet her thoughts and tune her mind, but eventually she could feel the magic of the Kazah Stone flare to life.

As it warmed her palm, a picture of her uncle emerged in Kendra's mind. She could see him sitting in a cell, his hands outstretched and his eyes closed in meditation. She could see each white whisker on his beard, could even hear his breathing.

Then Kendra felt the world around her begin to spin.

"She's going!" Oki cried.

"Grab her sleeve!" That was Gayla.

Kendra felt them clutch her arm and then—in a blinding flash of light—the spinning came to a stop. Kendra opened her eyes and blinked. They were still in the Elder Stone, in the exact same passage, but everything looked different. Now the dungeon cells were in pristine condition, set with rows of strong and sturdy bars, and the passageway was lit with flickering torches.

Kendra gazed down at the Kazah Stone. The crack seemed none the wider; but she wasn't sure. Tugging a braid, she returned the ring to her robe.

Gayla's wand was still glowing; she waved her hand to extinguish its light. "Are we in the right place?" she asked. "The cells are all here, but I don't see any prisoners."

"Maybe they're in a different row of cells," Kendra suggested.

"Hmph," Gayla grunted. "Or maybe you blundered the whole thing and dropped us in the wrong place."

"I think we're in the right place," Oki said timidly.

"Oh, yeah? And why's that?" Gayla demanded.

"Because I have a really bad feeling," Oki answered.

"You *always* have a bad feeling," Gayla retorted.

"Just leave him alone," Kendra said. "Come on, let's take a look around."

She led the way down the passage and almost immediately came to a dead end.

"Good job," Gayla said. "How are we supposed to rescue someone we can't find?"

"I don't get it," Kendra said. "Captain Ibb—and Kazah— brought us to this spot."

"Hmph," Gayla snorted. "I guess it's up to m—,"

But she didn't finish her sentence, for just then someone appeared at the end of the passageway. It was at that moment that Kendra knew she had succeeded in bringing them to the exact right time, for the Een now blocking their way was none other than her old enemy, Raggart Rinkle, Captain of the Een Guard. His nose and cheekbones flared red, sharp as spears, and as he snarled one jagged yellow tooth jutted from his mouth like an Unger's tusk. But most threatening was the long sword that he carried in one bony hand.

"Oy!" the hideous captain chuckled, his eyes gleaming ravenously at Kendra. "Ain't this a pleasant surprise. I thought you had done snuck out of Een for good. But you've come to the right place, dearie. My dungeons need filling."

"Take a look around, mirror-cracker," Gayla declared, stepping forward and raising her wand. "You're outnumbered."

Captain Rinkle tilted back his head and laughed, sending an echo down the corridor. Kendra couldn't help wondering what was so funny, but her answer came soon enough—for just then twelve Een soldiers turned the corner and took position behind the captain, each of them brandishing a weapon.

"Better count again," Captain Rinkle chortled. "This party be over."

CHAPTER 19

Gayla Goes on the Attack

Sometimes

the odds are stacked against us. This you'll know if you've ever played in an impor- tant game against a rival team that's bigger, faster, and stronger. You might feel like it's not even worth competing, that it might be better to just throw in the towel before the match even starts. You might feel like there's no hope—just like Kendra did at the moment she stared at Captain Rinkle and his guards.

Then something completely unex- pected happened.

Gayla lifted her head to the ceiling and unleashed a terrifying howl from her throat. It was the type of wild, savage howl that you might hear in the woods or from an animal at the zoo, the kind that sends a shiver scam- pering down your spine.

For a moment Captain Rinkle and his men froze, paralyzed by fear and surprise—but not for long. For in the next instant Gayla raised her wand and, still howling, charged. It didn't seem to matter that she was one against thirteen; she looked for all the world like an Unger on the hunt, and at once the Een guards turned tail and fled. Two or three of them even dropped their weapons. Around the corner they bolted, Gayla nipping at their heels with zaps from her wand.

Kendra listened in bafflement until the raucous sounds of the chase faded away. After a few seconds, she and Oki were left in complete silence, all alone at the dead end.

"*Holy kookamundo!* What just happened?" Oki exclaimed.

"She's crazy, that's what happened," Kendra said hotly. "But at least now we can look for Uncle Griffinskitch."

"And Ratchet," Oki added. "Remember, he's down here too."

"We'll find them both," Kendra assured him. "But I'm confused. We were brought to this specific spot in the dungeon. Shouldn't that mean we're close to them?"

Oki didn't answer. He was gazing intently at the dead-end wall.

"What is it?" Kendra asked.

"There's a long crack running up the stones," Oki said. "I may not know this part of the Elder Stone, but I know how the Elder Stone works. And I think there's a hidden door here." He scratched his whiskery chin and began pressing different stones on the wall. "Look," he said after a moment. "Up there—I can't reach it, but there's one stone a slightly different color. Push it, Kendra."

Kendra shrugged and pressed her hand against the rock. Just like that, the wall began to quietly shift to one side, revealing a long and narrow passageway faintly lit by a few torches. "Do you think that's where they are?" Kendra asked as she peered into the corridor.

"Your uncle's one of the most powerful wizards in Een," Oki remarked. "I'm guessing Burdock wanted to make it extra difficult for anyone to find him."

"Well, he never counted on you," Kendra said. "Come on."

They crept down the passageway, taking a few turns before coming to a sharp corner. Kendra felt her braids tingle. She paused, motioned Oki to be quiet, and peered around the stones to see a single cell set within the far wall. Sure enough, there was Uncle Griffinskitch. He was sitting in quiet meditation behind a row of thick wooden bars, eyes closed and arms extended, even though each wrist was cuffed in iron and shackled to the walls by heavy chains. He looked terribly pale and his long beard was streaked with grime.

Kendra stared at him in bewilderment. We must remember that the last time she had seen her uncle was in Gayla's time, when he was tall and intimidating. Now here he was, broken and ancient, like a wisp of white smoke against the cold stones of the dungeon. All at once Kendra realized how much she missed him, how much she wanted to save him.

Then, suddenly, Uncle Griffinskitch's eyes flew open. "Kendra?" he blurted.

How did he know I'm here? she wondered. She was just about to rush forward when he spoke again: "Mind your manners."

She froze.

"What does that mean?" Oki whispered.

Kendra shook her head. They waited. Then, from the shadows at the other end of the passage, a hunched and crooked figure strutted forward and stood before Uncle Grif-finskitch's cell.

"Burdock," Kendra gasped.

He was wearing a long, two-tailed coat, a fancy white scarf, and a pair of checkered trousers. In his flamboyant colors he looked completely out of place in the dismal dungeon.

"What did I hear you say?'" Burdock asked Uncle Grif-finskitch. "Kendra? Tut, tut, *old friend.* Do I look like that pesky girl? Perhaps your mind is going soft. I'm afraid your wayward niece has abandoned you—just like her mother, all those years ago. Unreliable sort, aren't they?"

Kendra felt her blood begin to boil. She had to fight the urge to jump out and blast Burdock with her wand.

"Humph," Uncle Griffinskitch grunted, glaring at Burdock.

"Oh, don't dismay," Burdock said in mock sympathy, wagging his staff at the white wizard. "You have me, after all. Don't I come and visit you each and every day?"

Just to taunt him, Kendra thought, yanking angrily on a braid.

"And look, I brought you something," Burdock announced. He reached into his coat and pulled out a staff. It was twisted and gnarled, much longer than Burdock's own wand; Kendra recognized it at once as her uncle's. Burdock twirled it in front of Uncle Griffinskitch and smiled smugly. "I thought you might like to gaze upon it," Burdock jeered. "I'd let you have it, you know—if only you had picked your sides better."

"I would rather side with a skerpent," Uncle Griffinskitch growled.

"Careful what you wish for—skerpents can be arranged," Burdock snarled.

"Oki," Kendra whispered ever so softly as Burdock and her uncle began a heated exchange of words. "We have to snatch that staff."

"How?" Oki asked.

"You sneak behind Burdock," Kendra said. "Once you're close enough I'll distract him, make him drop it—then you grab the staff and get it to Uncle Griffinskitch."

"Me?" Oki asked. "Why don't you do the sneaking?"

"You're smaller," Kendra explained. "He probably won't see you."

"Probably?" Oki squeaked.

"You can do it," Kendra said. "Just don't think of eggs."

Oki sighed, but with a nervous twitch of his tail crept around the corner.

Kendra glanced at Uncle Griffinskitch; if he noticed Oki, his face betrayed no surprise. As for Burdock, he had his back to the little mouse. Slowly and carefully, Oki maneuvered along the wall until he was just a tail's length away from Burdock.

Kendra gave her friend a reassuring nod and, with one final tug on a braid, slipped the Kazah Stone onto her finger and stepped boldly around the corner. Burdock heard her at once and whirled around.

"Well, well," he growled, raising his staff at Kendra. "If it isn't the braided brat. You are no match for me, Eenling. Hand over your wand and maybe I'll allow you to bade farewell to your uncle before I lock you away."

"Oh, I have something much better than a wand," Kendra announced, raising her hand to show the decrepit old wizard the Kazah Stone.

"Agent Lurk's ring!" Burdock exclaimed. "Where did you get that?"

"I'm more powerful than you think," Kendra declared. "Don't you know what this is? It's a Kazah Stone."

"How do you know about Kazah?" Burdock demanded, thumping his staff on the floor. "Only fully-trained wizards are introduced to such mysteries."

"Like I said," Kendra proclaimed. "I'm more powerful than you think. I know all about Kazah. Have you ever seen one this round, Burdock? This is the most powerful Kazah Stone in all the world."

"So you say," Burdock sneered. But his beady eyes gleamed with lust.

"I'll give it to you," Kendra said, keeping half an eye on Oki as he took one careful step closer to Burdock. "Just free my uncle."

"You're in no position to negotiate," Burdock snarled. "I'll take what I please."

"If that's the way you're going to be, I'll just give you the ring," Kendra said. "Here—catch!"

She pretended to throw it in the air—greedily, Burdock reached for it—but to do so, he had to drop Uncle Griffinskitch's staff. Many things now seemed to happen at once. Kendra raised her own wand and sent a zap in Burdock's direction. It wasn't much, but it struck the hunched wizard in the shoulder and sent him staggering back a step. At that exact moment, Oki scurried forward and snatched Uncle Griffinskitch's staff, just as it clattered to the ground. Quickly, he slid it through the bars of the cell and into the wizard's waiting hands.

In an instant, Uncle Griffinskitch had freed himself of his chains. He waved his staff, tore a gaping hole in his bars, and barreled towards Burdock, who was just regaining his wits.

Kendra saw Burdock's eyes fly open in surprise, but instead of firing back, the hunched wizard merely aimed his wand at the ceiling and, with a fiery burst of lightning, brought down an avalanche of stone.

"Run!" Kendra screamed.

Desperately, she swung her wand to summon a protection spell—but she was too slow. A stone struck her in the chest and sent her sprawling backwards. What few torches were lighting the tunnel were now extinguished in the collapse of the ceiling; the last thing Kendra saw before she was cast into darkness was the sight of Burdock Brown, skittering away to safety, like a spider.

CHAPTER 20

Troubles and Traps

Kendra couldn't see—but she could hear. The sound of the rocks falling was thunderous. Still on her back, the tiny Een girl pulled herself back on her elbows, desperately hoping that none of the tumbling stones would crush her. She felt giant, angular slabs of rock smashing the nearby ground, but the next thing she knew silence returned. The calamity was over.

Kendra sat up and waved her hand over the top of her wand, trying to coax light from it. She could only muster the faintest glow.

"Kendra?" came a timid voice.

"Oki?" Kendra picked her way across the broken rock and found him with his tail pinched beneath a stone. She put her shoulder against it and rolled it away. "Are you okay?" she asked.

He nodded. "Where's Burdock?"

"Fled like a coward," she answered. "We have to find my uncle."

Together, they stumbled over the rubble and called out for the old wizard. Then Kendra heard a cough, and knew it was him. She moved towards the sound, but soon bumped against a wall of rock. The ceiling had fallen in such a way as to divide the passageway completely in two, with Uncle Griffinskitch on one side and they on the other. Kendra raised her glowing wand to the barrier of rock, finding only a small chink.

"Uncle Griffinskitch?" she called. "Are you okay?"

In a moment the old wizard's face appeared in the gap. He was trembling and perspiration was pouring down his rigid face. He was completely spent, Kendra realized. Weeks of imprisonment with lack of proper food and sleep, combined with his sudden outburst of magic, had drained him.

"Can you get out from your side?" Kendra asked.

"Aye," the old wizard replied. "There is a secret door over here, the one Burdock used to escape. How about you?"

"I think we can go back the way we came," Kendra replied.

"Then we'll meet up in the dungeon complex," Uncle Griffinskitch directed. "In the meantime, we can communicate through our wands."

Kendra shook her head. "You have to go without us. The thing you must worry about is finding the Rumble Pit."

"Rumble Pit?" Uncle Griffinskitch asked. "Where is that? And why would I want to go there?"

"Because," Kendra persisted. "I'm there. And you need to save me."

Uncle Griffinskitch stared at her through the chink in the rock, his eyes flickering in confusion. "But you're here. How can you be in two places at once?"

Kendra raised her hand and showed him the Kazah Stone.
"Days of Een," the old wizard gasped. "Can it be true? A
Kazah Stone powerful enough to enable a leap through time?"

Kendra nodded. She told him everything . . . well, most
things. She couldn't tell him about Gayla, or meeting her
elderly self—she didn't even know how to begin explaining
that situation.

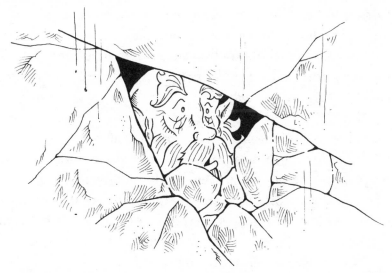

What she did tell him was that he needed to find Ratchet,
escape the dungeons, and meet up with Professor Bumblebean. She told him about Ratchet's cloud ship and how Winter Woodsong could help them escape through the magic curtain, even though Burdock had sealed it. She described to him
the terrors of the Rumble Pit, and how she was a prisoner
there, along with Trooogul. She explained about the giant
queen of the Krakes, and how she laid hundreds of eggs in her
royal hatchery. Lastly, she told him about the peryton, that
magnificent winged deer, and how he would be injured and
dying in the pit.

"You must come prepared to save the peryton," Kendra emphasized. "Save the peryton and you save me."

Through the crack in the rocks, Kendra saw Uncle Griffinskitch stroke his long whiskers. "Humph," he said at long last. It wasn't a normal humph, Kendra knew. It was the type of humph that meant . . . well, it meant that he didn't know what else to say. She had just told him a pretty implausible story, after all. But Kendra knew he believed it. Even in the dim light, she could see it in his eyes.

Then Uncle Griffinskitch reached a trembling hand through the gap in the rock and touched Kendra's cheek. "Your bangs are too long," he grunted.

"I haven't exactly had time for a haircut," she said.

"Humph. Sometimes you remind me all too much of—,"

He didn't finish his sentence; just then a clamor could be heard from the dungeon. Kendra glanced over her shoulder. The sound was coming from her side of the rock barrier, and she realized at once it was the return of Captain Rinkle and his men. They were shouting and clanging their swords.

"We have to go," Kendra announced.

"Aye," Uncle Griffinskitch said. "I will see you at the Rumble Pit. I promise." Through the crack, he looked sharply at Oki. "Look after her, Honest One." Then, in an instant, he was gone.

Kendra suddenly realized a tear had snuck down her cheek. She almost envied the Kendra that was trapped in the Rumble Pit. That Kendra was going to see Uncle Griffinskitch soon enough. But what about her? When would she see him again?

There was no time to dwell on the matter. They began moving down the passage, back the way they had originally come. There were torches in the wall ahead so it wasn't as dark, but many of the rocks had tumbled far down the corridor. It was like navigating a mountain pass.

"I think they're headed straight towards us," Oki fretted as the sounds of approaching footsteps grew louder.

But the first Een they encountered was Gayla; she came sprinting around a curve in the passage with such speed that she nearly collided into them.

"You're hurt!" Oki exclaimed.

He was right. Gayla had a gash on one cheek and another on her shoulder; blood was trickling in a long curl down her arm and dripping from her wand hand.

"It's nothing," the wild girl panted.

"What happened?" Kendra asked.

"I chased those scaredy-skulls all the way to another dead end," Gayla said. "Then they realized they outnumbered me and came back swinging. What about you?"

"We found Unc—my master," Kendra replied. "We were separated, but he's free and on his way."

"Good," Gayla said. "Now we just have to make like an egg and scramble out of here!"

"Not so easy," Kendra told her. "It's blocked behind us."

"Great," Gayla muttered. "We're in trouble. Better take cover."

They crouched behind one of the broken slabs of stone that had fallen from the ceiling, just as Captain Rinkle and the Een soldiers appeared. Gayla peered over and sent a warning zap in their direction, but it was a weak one. Kendra could see that her magic was exhausted. She was only an apprentice too, after all. A spear whistled over their heads.

"Hmph," Gayla grunted. She picked up a small, fist-sized stone, jumped up, and flung it at the oncoming swarm of Een

guards. Kendra heard one of them wail in pain, and the entire company seemed to screech to a halt.

Gayla ducked back down, her eyes wide with panic. "Th-there's . . . I think it's . . . "

"What?" Kendra said. She peeked out from behind the boulder. There were only six or seven Een soldiers left, and many of them looked worse for wear. Even Captain Rinkle was kneeling on the ground, seemingly nursing a black eye. Then she saw what had shocked Gayla. "Burdock!" Kendra gasped.

"Eek!" Oki cried. "He came back."

"He's older," Gayla gasped, leaning against the back of the boulder. "And uglier."

Then the hideous wizard spoke. "Surrender!" he cried.

"Go for it—we accept!" Gayla screamed over her shoulder. "Not us—*you!*"

Gayla looked down at Kendra. "So much for *that* plan. You still got the Kazah Stone?"

Kendra raised her finger.

"Time to use it," Gayla said.

"How am I going to concentrate when we're under attack?" Kendra asked.

"I don't know," Gayla said. "But you're going to have to try. Eeks and I will hold off these snot-suckers."

"Oh, don't think of eggs!" Oki agonized.

"Where should we go?" Kendra asked.

"Anywhere!" Gayla screeched. "Somewhere where there's no Burdock!"

"Or Ungers," Oki added. "Or Goojuns, or . . . "

Kendra tuned him out. She tucked her wand into her belt, closed her eyes, and raised the Kazah Stone. She tried to concentrate, tried to focus and mute the sounds of the passage-way.

No Burdock! she thought. *No Ungers, no Goojuns . . .*

She tried to imagine a place of peace. A place of serenity. No war. No terror. Then she thought of water. Yes, it was calming. She imagined the sound of bubbles, the cool feeling against her skin. She imagined the smell of it.

Faintly, one corner of her mind heard someone—Captain Rinkle?—yell, "Charge!"

Go back, Kendra told herself desperately. *Days of Een! Just take me back, back, back, back . . .*

Then the Kazah Stone must have started to work, for Kendra suddenly felt Gayla and Oki clutch her sleeve. Then, in a flash, they were gone.

CHAPTER 21

A Plunge into the Past

Something

was wrong. It was like all of Kendra's senses were clogged; she couldn't quite see or hear or move. It was cold, and her nose was stinging as if someone had punched her. She opened her mouth to scream and water flooded down her throat. In an instant of terror she realized what was happening.

She was drowning.

Frantically Kendra waved her arms, but she was disoriented and didn't know which way was which. Then she felt something grab her by two braids and yank her upwards, hard. Next it was a hand underneath each arm. She broke the surface with a gasp and was dragged onto a grassy bank. She lay there heaving, and it was only after a few seconds that she had recovered enough strength to look over and gaze upon her rescuer. It was Gayla. She looked in just as bad shape as Kendra, dripping wet and breathing heavily.

"Oki?" Kendra gasped, suddenly realizing he was missing.

Gayla's eyes flashed with alarm and she plunged back into the water. Kendra crawled to the edge, panicking; but only a moment later Gayla reappeared, this time clutching a very soggy mouse. Kendra reached out and helped pull them both to shore, and there all three of them lay for several minutes, coughing up water in shock and exhaustion.

"Where are we?" Gayla asked finally, sitting up. "Shouldn't we have just landed back in the Elder Stone, but in a different time?"

Kendra nodded. She pulled herself to her elbows and took a look at their surroundings. They were at the edge of a large, round pond in the middle of the woods, but nothing seemed familiar. "There's definitely no Elder Stone here," Kendra said.

"Good job, Braids," Gayla snorted. "Not only do we not know *when* we are—now we don't know *where*. Figure out how to use that Stone before you kill us!"

Kendra wiggled the ring off her finger and held it in her palm. "The crack is getting wider," she murmured.

"What does that mean?" Gayla asked.

"The blind old sorceress warned me about it," Kendra replied. "We have to be careful . . . too many jumps and the Kazah Stone will burst completely apart."

"Eek!" Oki squealed. "Maybe it already stopped working. Maybe that's why it brought us . . . well, *here*."

"Hmph," Gayla grunted.

"Your arm is still bleeding," Kendra said, now tucking the ring in her pocket. "We have to get you fixed up."

"It's just a scratch," Gayla told her, though she grimaced as she spoke.

Kendra was just about to insist upon taking a closer look at her injury when a slight movement caught her eye, and she turned to see a rust-colored squirrel sitting at the edge of the pond, just a short distance away. It was staring at her with two large, round eyes.

Kendra assumed at once that the squirrel was an Een, for though he wore no clothes, he was very large. (Een animals, of course, are much bigger than the normal critters we find in our backyards or out in the woods.)

"Hello," Kendra said to the squirrel. "Can you tell us where we are?"

The squirrel cocked its head quizzically at Kendra and then broke out in a chatter: "Chy chy chee chee! Chee chee chasta!"

Kendra looked at Oki and Gayla in surprise. "He can't talk! Maybe he *is* wild after all."

The squirrel chattered again, this time in a more excited manner, his fluffy tail twitching back and forth like a flag.

"Hmm," Oki murmured.

He stepped closer to the squirrel and then, much to Kendra's amazement, chattered back. This exchange went on between the two animals for some time until at last Gayla said, "Hey, Eeks! Can you actually understand Chatterbox?"

"Sort of," Oki replied. "He's speaking . . . well, it's like an ancient dialect or something. I don't quite understand. It's like he's trying to speak, but he can't quite do it. I think he *is* an Een squirrel."

"Then that means we *are* in Een," Kendra said. "But the question is *when?*"

Gayla shook her head and looked back at Oki. "Well, what did that little twitter-tail say?" she asked.

"I'm not sure," Oki answered. "I think he wants us to follow him . . . to his *dray.* I think he means his family . . . or his house."

"Well," Gayla muttered, wincing as she climbed to her feet. "We don't have anything better to do. Maybe he's got some acorn soup on the go. I don't know about you two drips, but I'm starving."

This remark seemed to quite please the squirrel, and he now beckoned them to follow him through the woods. It was warm at least; Kendra guessed it was either late spring or early summer, and the walk helped dry them even further. As for the squirrel, he scampered far ahead, sometimes scrambling up tree trunks and leaping from one low-hanging branch to another. It took some effort for Kendra and the others to keep up, but after an hour or so they reached a clearing with a small knoll in the center. The knoll was shaped like the wave of the sea, and from its crest there grew a long, crooked tree; this was definitely an Een house, for it had doors and windows and even a small chimney pipe. Indeed, it quite reminded Kendra of her own house.

The squirrel led them along a cobblestone path that wound up the knoll, but before they even reached the house the front door swung open and there stood a tall and elderly

Een. He was an imposing figure, with a giant, blunt nose and large ears. He had a long, white beard and even longer locks of snow-white hair that curled at his feet. In one hand he held a knotted staff of Eenwood. There was no doubt he was a wizard—the type, Kendra thought, you didn't want to mess with.

Then the wizard spoke, and at once completely changed Kendra's opinion. "Ah, Clovin, my furry friend!" he trilled in a voice that sounded altogether musical. "You've found our visitors. *Fabullation!*"

"Fabullation?" Oki squeaked.

The wizard looked down at the mouse in surprise. "Did you just speak?" he asked.

"Er . . . yes?" Oki answered timidly.

"Fabullation indeed!" the wizard exclaimed. "A most appropriate word on this momentous occasion! A mouse that can speak! And you do it as well as any poet!"

"A poet?" Gayla snorted in derision. "Do you want to hear him recite *Ode to Eggs?*"

The old wizard tilted his head back and released a hearty laugh. "Indeed—I would!" he declared. "And you two kind sisters," he added, gazing intently upon Kendra and Gayla. "What wondrous braids you have!"

"Er . . . we're not sisters," Kendra told him. "We're just, sort of—,"

"Thrown together right now," Gayla interjected.

"Aha!" the wizard cried. "Well, come, come. We must sup. But first, let's get you refreshed and repaired; it seems as if you"—here, he looked pointedly at Gayla's bleeding arm—"have had some adventure."

He chattered something to Clovin (which was what the squirrel's name seemed to be), and the bushy-tailed creature at once ushered the three companions into the house. The inside was very similar to Kendra's own home, for the rooms were narrow and cozy, and everywhere Kendra looked there was another nook crammed with books, scrolls, and mysterious instruments.

Clovin led them up a steep corkscrew staircase to a small room that contained a washbasin, a trunk, and a shelf filled with an assortment of bottles. Clovin pulled a roll of cloth from the trunk, yattered something to Oki, and with a nod scampered back down the stairs.

"There's medicine in those bottles," Oki translated. "And we can use this cloth for a bandage."

"Ugh," Gayla snorted as she uncapped one of the bottles to take a sniff. "Smells like Goojun breath. I'm not putting any of this stinky-pink on my arm."

"Just let me clean and bandage you," Kendra said, rolling her eyes.

"You know," Gayla said, taking a seat on the trunk so that Kendra could begin washing her wound, "that's one strange old man. I'm sure I've seen him somewhere before."

"Of course you have," Oki declared. "We just saw him. Well, at least in statue form."

"What—OW!" Gayla snapped, flinching as Kendra administered the medicine. "Careful. That hurts. What in the name of Een are you talking about, Eeks?"

"We've traveled *way* back," Oki explained. "That wizard is Leemus Longbraids, one of the very first elders!"

"Days of Een!" Kendra cried, looking up in surprise.

"Exactly," Oki said. "We're visiting ancient history. Before Een animals could talk, or before there even was such a thing as Een animals. Before there was a magic curtain. Before the building of the Elder Stone—that's why we landed in the pond. There is *no* Elder Stone in this time!"

"Are you telling me the fuddy-duddy downstairs is that wizard from all those boring legends?" Gayla asked. "I thought those stories were all just made up."

"Oh, they're real," Oki said. "Take Clovin. Haven't you heard how Een animals came to be? They were wild once, but after living with Eens, they started to absorb their magic. They started to change. That's what's happening to Clovin right now—he's learning to talk, he's . . . well, he's *Eening.*"

"But if that's Leemus, where are his braids?" Kendra wondered. "He didn't have any."

"I know," Oki said, furling his brow. "That *is* strange. But it's him all right."

"Hmph," Gayla murmured thoughtfully. "Krimson would pluck out his eyebrows to be here right now. He's always going on about all that mythology stuff. Wait until I tell him our founding father was a crazy old coot."

"Leemus Longbraids is not a crazy old coot," Kendra said as she began bandaging Gayla's arm. "He was—well, *is*—the wisest of Eens. And I like him."

"Me too," Oki added.

"Of course you do," Gayla told the mouse. "He uses silly words."

"Like fabullation," Oki said. "Ratchet and I can put that one in the dictionary."

"I've got some words for you," Gayla offered. "How about Egghead? Fur-nerd? Eek-geek?"

"Just drop it," Kendra said in exasperation, as she finished up Gayla's arm. "We've got bigger worries than silly words. What are we supposed to do now?"

"Eat dinner," Gayla replied, for just then Clovin had reappeared at the doorway. "Let's just hope that old man knows how to cook."

CHAPTER 22

Leemus Longshanks and the Brothers of Een

You never know what to expect when you are asked to dinner, especially when going to someone's house for the first time. Of course, you might think a wizard would be capable of whipping up a grand and delicious feast with a mere flick of his staff, but the truth is that while Een wizards are known for many things, cooking is not one of them. This is why Kendra wasn't the least bit surprised to discover that dinner was nothing more than Squibbles and Pip (or, as we might call it—leftovers).

"I hope you will excuse my humble offerings," Leemus said as everyone took a seat at the table. "Visitors such as you certainly deserve a scrumptious feast. But I am a simple wizard, after all."

161

161

Clovin chittered in the wizard's ear, causing him to exclaim, "Oh my! It seems that in all the fuddle-duddle I failed to make proper introductions. This is Clovin, my loyal assistant. As for me, I am Leemus Longshanks, a brother of the Lands of—,"

"Longshanks?" Gayla interrupted as she began spooning some of the Squibbles and Pip onto her plate (it looked rather like mashed potatoes). "Don't you mean Longbraids?"

"*Toodlewitches!*" the wizard exclaimed. "I think I know my own name."

"Well, you are the *wise* one," Gayla snorted, and Kendra felt it was such a rude remark that she tried to kick her under the table. Unfortunately, she booted Oki instead, causing the mouse to squeal and drop his fork.

"Now, now," Leemus said. "There's no need to get in a *frunzy!* Are you all right, my little friend?"

Oki nodded, and Kendra whispered him a "sorry." Then she thought to herself, *Longshanks? How could all the stories and legends get his name wrong? But he doesn't have braids, that's for sure.*

"Well, come, come, my friends," Leemus said, interrupting Kendra's musings. "It's time to tell me *your* names."

"Sure," Gayla said between bites. "This is Braids and Eeks—or Kendra and Oki, if you like. And I'm Gayla. We're from . . . well, let's just say *far away.*"

"Far away indeed," Leemus mused, leaning back to stroke his beard. "Clovin tells me you came swimming from the sacred Elder Pool."

"Well, some of us were swimming," Gayla said, casting a sidelong glance at Kendra and Oki. "Others were drowning."

"Er . . . we didn't mean to be in the Elder Pool," Kendra told Leemus. "We just ended up there by accident."

"I see, I see," Leemus mused, now twisting one finger around the tail of his beard. "Such are the dangers of celestial travel, I suppose."

"What is that supposed to mean?" Gayla asked.

"I have been studying the heavens these many months," Leemus replied. "The stars have foretold that travelers from the great beyond would arrive at my doorstep—and now, here you are. Why, I suppose you are Eengels!"

Kendra, who had just taken a drink of Eenberry juice, nearly spit it out in surprise (actually, she was lucky it didn't come out of her nose). Eengels, of course, are what you and I might call angels. Kendra had been called many things in her life—but Eengel had never been one of them.

"You've got your whiskers crossed," Gayla told Leemus. "We're not Eengels! We're Eens. Just like you."

"*Smingle-smongle!*" Leemus scoffed. "You are no ordinary Eens! You have been sent to help us; this I know. And tonight I shall take you to meet my brothers at the Elder Stone."

Kendra looked at the wizard in surprise. "But there is no . . . er, well, that is to say: where is the Elder Stone?"

"Why, right next to the Elder Pool," Leemus answered. "Didn't you see it? Well, you shall tonight; all in good time."

"But what's going to happen at the meeting?" Oki asked.

The old wizard's face suddenly turned serious. "Tonight the council meets to discuss our brother . . . the fallen one."

Kendra shivered. She knew Leemus was speaking of the first elder of Een, Grendel Greeve. He was a dark wizard, and she had met him—well, his ghost at least—in the temple he had built with the power of his black arts, so many years ago. *Except it's not years ago,* Kendra thought. *It's all happening right now—and we're in the middle of it.*

"The heart of Brother Greeve turned so dark and wicked that we banished him from our lands," Leemus said, a tone of regret clear in his voice. "That was three years ago. And yet, seven moons past, a giant moth appeared before the council, carrying in its feelers a message from our brother, begging for forgiveness. Tonight we shall decide our response."

Kendra tugged hard on a braid. She knew how this was going to turn out. The brothers would go before the Wizard Greeve and all would fall victim to his curse—all except Leemus.

Maybe I can convince the elders not to go, Kendra thought. *I can stop this curse from even happening.* But then another voice came to her. It sounded like her elder self, the blind sorceress. *You cannot pull at the fabric of time, Kendra,* the voice warned. *If you do, everything will change.*

Kendra sighed and stared across the table at Leemus. *He thinks we've been sent to help him,* Kendra told herself. *And he's said to be the wisest Een that's ever lived. So there must be something we have to do in this time. The question is . . . what?*

The moon had just appeared in the sky when the three "Eengels" set off for the council meeting, following Leemus Longshanks along the same path in the woods that they had taken earlier that day. Clovin scampered through the treetops above, leaping gracefully from branch to branch.

It wasn't long before they began clambering down a slope and the Elder Pool came into view. Now that she was looking at the meadow from above, Kendra could see a large, flat stone lying near the pool. Here, sitting cross-legged around the perimeter of the rock, were five dark silhouettes.

"I guess those are the Brothers of Een," Kendra said to Oki. "And that must be the Elder Stone."

"I recognize that rock," Oki told her excitedly. "It's the center tile in the council chambers of *our* Elder Stone."

"That makes sense," Kendra said. "The ancients must have used that rock when they built the new Elder Stone."

They arrived at the bottom of the slope, and as they approached the stone Kendra was afforded a better view of the five brothers. She already knew their names: Izzen Icebone, Nooja Nightstorm, Orin Oldhorn, Drake Dragonclaw, and Thunger Thunderfist. They did not look kind in Kendra's opinion, especially Brother Thunderfist, who was massive in size with a hunched back and two fists like rocks. Like Leemus, none of them wore braids in their hair.

"You're telling me they're brothers?" Gayla asked. "They all look completely different."

"Oh, they're not actually related," Oki explained. "There's one legend that tells how the first seven elders took an oath that bound them as one. 'Brother' is just a title. You know, like 'Elder.'"

"How about the title of 'I-don't-actually-give-an-eek'?" Gayla muttered.

Kendra would have had a retort for her, but Leemus escorted them onto the Elder Stone and directly into the circle of brothers. All eyes were upon them; Oki began murmuring about eggs and Kendra had to nudge him to be quiet.

"What now, Brother Longshanks?" asked Izzen Icebone, some amusement in his voice as he stared at Kendra's hair. "Is it not enough that you always insist on bringing your bushy-tailed sidekick to our council meetings? Tell us, who are these strangers?"

"My brothers, a most *splendulous* event has occurred," Leemus declared, his arms wheeling in the air as he spoke. "The Eengels we have been awaiting have arrived."

"We?" asked Drake Dragonclaw, his quizzical expression punctuated by a crop of spiky hair. "You, Brother Longshanks, are the only one who has foretold these so-called Eengels."

Kendra fussed nervously with a braid. It didn't sound like Leemus was exactly the most popular member of the council.

"I shall prove they are from beyond," the long-haired wizard declared. "Listen: the mouse can speak."

He pushed Oki forward and, after much prodding, convinced him to talk.

"Spells and witchcraft for all we know," Nooja Nightstorm grunted after Oki had forced out a few words. "What—if anything—is so special about these two sisters?"

"We're not sisters," Gayla interjected, crossing her arms.

Kendra, embarrassed by her rudeness, reached up to tug another braid; her palm must have shown in the moonlight, for at once Thunger Thunderfist cried, "Wait, child. Show your hand again."

Kendra slowly raised her palm. The brothers gasped.

"Look!" Leemus declared. "She has the mark."

Kendra gazed down at her own hand—it was nothing she could see, but she knew the mark was there. In her time, it was something only the Ungers and other monster tribes could see. For them it was part of a prophecy, that she would destroy the Door to Unger. And, of course, she had.

166

Now, in the ancient past, the mark seemed important again. When she looked away from her palm, she saw that all six brothers had raised their hands. She could see nothing on their palms—but it was clear that they could.

"When we took our oath as brothers, the mark appeared," Orin Oldhorn declared. "It is a sign of unity and purity. But the question is, why do *you* have it, child?"

Kendra gulped. What was she supposed to say? She had just been born with it. She couldn't explain why. And she couldn't tell them about the future either, not anything specific anyway. But the brothers were staring at her expectantly, so she just blurted out, "It is as you say. It is a sign of . . . purity. It means that I am the destroyer of the Door to . . . well, a door to darkness and doom."

"A door to darkness and doom?" Nooja scoffed. "What door? I know of no such thing."

"You will," Kendra assured him.

"You!" Thunger Thunderfist growled in an accusatory tone. "You predict our future, do you?"

167

Kendra fidgeted.

"Bah!" Thunger growled with a dismissive wave of an enormous hand. "How can we trust these strangers? Perhaps they have been sent here by Brother Greeve himself. They could be part of an elaborate plot to betray us."

"No!" Kendra cried. "We're on your side . . . I assure you."

For a moment no one said anything; Kendra thought she might melt by their icy stares.

At last Izzen Icebone spoke: "There is no doubt that the arrival of these three strangers presents some mystery, and we know not if they be friend or foe. I suggest we decide their fate once we have turned our minds to the matter at hand: the invitation from Grendel Greeve."

There was a murmur of consensus from the brothers. Kendra, Gayla, and Oki were asked to leave the stone, and Clovin escorted them to a nearby tree, where a low-hanging branch served as a type of bench.

"You know," Oki whispered, "there's no Captain of the Guard here . . . no reason why we just can't use Kazah and escape while we can."

"Escape?" Gayla asked. "From what? These moldy-oldies? They're not out to hurt us, Eeks. Let's just listen in on what they have to say."

"I thought you didn't care about all of this legend stuff," Kendra said.

Gayla's only response was a disgruntled "hmph," so with a sigh, Kendra leaned forward, strained her ears, and listened to the words of the first elders of Een.

CHAPTER 23

In the Company of Thunger Thunderfist

Drake Dragonclaw now raised his staff in the moonlight and with some formality announced, "Tonight we hold council to decide our response to the plea of our fallen brother. We shall begin by hearing once again his letter so that his words are fresh in our minds. Brother Nightstorm, the letter is in your possession. Please read it for us now."

Nooja Nightstorm nodded and reached into his tunic to produce a small roll of parchment. After fiddling with his spectacles, he read:

Brothers,

I write with the humblest of hearts to entreat your forgiveness. I tell you all in earnest, I am an Een transformed. Wandering in exile, lo these many years, has washed away the treachery of my heart. Hear me, brothers! It is with ardent joy that I tell you I am

169

like a garden which flourishes without weeds. Listen: I have built a sanctuary in the wilderness, a palace of peace amidst beauty and bounty. I call it Greeve's Green, and I beseech you to visit me, to be my noble guests. The stars shall direct you; come to me, my brothers. Let the brotherhood be whole again.

With all humility,
Your Brother Greeve

Kendra listened to all of this in wonder. *Greeve's Green?* she thought. She had been there—it had been anything but green. In her time, it was called the Greeven Wastes, a desolate place of rock and ruin. It was here that the dark temple had stood, guarded by the Door to Unger, the very one she had destroyed—well, in the future, at least. She shuddered to think of it in *this* time, standing newly erected.

The council was now silent. Kendra looked over at Gayla, and noticed her staring intently at the circle of wizards. Kendra wondered what was going through her mind.

Finally, Thunger Thunderfist cleared his throat. "This message fills me with terrible unease," he declared. "I do not trust the words of our fallen brother. I have spent many sleepless nights considering our path forward, and this is what I propose. Let us, indeed, journey to Greeve's Green, to meet our brother. But let us take Eens armed with spear and sword, so that we might be prepared against his further betrayal."

"An army?!" Leemus cried (he was now sitting, having taken a place between Thunger and Izzen). "What *ticklewickle* is this?" he demanded. "My brothers, I implore you. War is not the way of Eens."

"Nor is treachery and darkness," Drake said. "Yet these are the traits demonstrated by our fallen brother. I, for one, agree with Brother Thunderfist's plan. We go not to make war, but to guard ourselves against danger."

The other brothers now broke out in heated debate, but at last Izzen was able to quiet them. "Enough!" he boomed, banging his staff against the Elder Stone. "Each of us has contemplated this for seven moons: long enough. Let us put it to vote. Who supports the plan put forth by Brother Thunderfist?"

Three hands immediately went to the air. After a moment, two more joined them. Only Leemus did not agree with the decision.

"The council has spoken," Izzen proclaimed. "Let us make arms and in three moons set forth to meet with our fallen brother. It will take us several weeks to reach the palace of the Wizard Greeve. It will be an onerous journey, but hopefully a fruitful one."

"And what of the Eengels?" Leemus asked. "Should we not consult them? They have come from the beyond to give us counsel in these most *gindly* times."

"I do not know what to make of these strange Eens," Izzen said. "Perhaps they are for us; perhaps not. So let them accompany us to Greeve's Green. This way they shall never leave our watchful eye. We shall know their purpose yet."

"What shall we do with them in the meantime?" Nooja asked.

"Split them up," Thunger declared. "That way, they shall have no chance to confer or plot. I shall take the younger sister. Nooja can take the other. As for the mouse . . . why, Leemus, you so relish the company of critters. The mouse stays with you."

"They are not our prisoners!" Leemus exclaimed, rising to his feet.

"Sit, Brother," Izzen hissed. "Indeed, they are *not* prisoners, and we shall not treat them as such. But they shall not meet or speak to one another during these next three days, nor during the journey itself. These are troubled times, and we must take caution."

"We're in a *wongle* now," Oki moaned from their tree branch. "See!? We should have left when we had the chance. Now we have to go back to the Door to Unger! Oh, don't think of eggs! Don't think of eggs!"

"What do you mean *back?*" Gayla snapped. "What is this Door anyway? And this mark on your hand, Braids? There's a whole lot you little sneaky snirtles haven't told me and I want answers."

Kendra yanked hard on her braid. Luckily, she didn't have to come up with an answer, for just then Thunger Thunderfist lumbered over to her and with one mighty hand scooped her from the tree branch and led her away. She cast a frantic look over her shoulder and managed a wave to her companions. She was thankful Oki was staying with Leemus and Clovin. She could only imagine how panicked he would be to be put under the watchful eye of the giant Thunger Thunderfist.

Like her.

We're in trouble, she told herself as she walked in the enormous shadow that Thunger cast in the moonlight. *I can't jump time while we're split up. That would mean abandoning Gayla and Oki. And now we have to go back to the Door to Unger. The Wizard Greeve is going to curse the elders—and us, too.*

There have probably been times when your friends or family have become embroiled in a fight, causing you to endure some long and uncomfortable silence over dinner or on the ride home. For Kendra, the next three days were exactly like this. She could tell both the temper and anxiety of Thunger Thunderfist were high, and the giant wizard spoke only to give her the simplest of commands.

Kendra caught him looking at her palm from time to time, trying to glimpse the mark, but he never directly asked her about it again. She supposed he simply did not trust her. And so she was confined to his house (a humble abode, in a hollowed-out ledge of rock) and spent her hours meditating by a small crack that served as a window. She could not see the preparation of the Een army, but she could often hear it. The sounds of weapon-making filled her ears: the smash of hammers against metal and the sharpening of stone.

After three days, early in the morning, Thunger roused her from the hammock he had strung for her in one corner of the cave-like dwelling. After a simple breakfast, Kendra followed the wizard to the edge of a vast field, where she

estimated over one hundred and fifty Eens had assembled. They were divided into regiments, each marked by different colored uniforms and flags to represent the brother that commanded them (Thunger's men wore gray and brown). There were also many women attached to each regiment; Kendra could tell by their garb and supplies that they were the cooks and messengers of the army. But for the most part the field was full of men, each of them burdened with heavy weapons: swords, axes, and spears.

An entire army of Eens, Kendra thought in wonder. *The history books never said anything about this.*

Try as she might, Kendra could catch no glimpse of Oki or Gayla, though she did at one point see Leemus. His regiment was clothed in uniforms of forest green, and even Clovin was wearing a long cape that fluttered in the morning breeze.

I guess he's coming, too, Kendra thought, but he was the only animal in the entire assemblage (other than Oki, whom she hoped was somewhere).

Then, with a wave of his staff, Izzen Icebone gave the order for the massive army to march. And march they did.

"You," Thunger said to Kendra, putting a sturdy hand on her shoulder. "You will not leave my sight."

Kendra nodded. She still had no idea what part she was meant to play in all of this. Was she meant to stop the curse? Was she meant to save Leemus from it? Then she heard once again the voice of the blind old sorceress, her elder self. It reverberated in her mind, clearly as if she was standing right next to her: *Surrender, Kendra,* the voice said. *Trust.*

Kendra trudged forward and pulled on a braid. *Easily said,* she told herself. *Much harder to do.*

CHAPTER 24

Treachery in the Palace of Peace

The next few weeks were lonely ones for Kendra. Thunger Thunderfist was ever present, but he continued to be a wall of stony silence. She tried engaging some of the cooks and messengers in conversation, but a rumor had gone through the army that she was either Eengel or spy, and most were too spooked to offer the Een girl much more than a hasty nod.

She saw very little of Oki and Gayla during this time. If she was lucky, she would catch a glimpse of them, but she was never allowed to speak to them, or even get close enough to exchange a hand signal. On the luckiest of days, Clovin would scamper up and chatter something in her ear. She always hoped it was a message from Oki, but she could never understand the squirrel.

And so time moved slowly, each day the same as the last: wake up, eat, break camp, march, eat, make camp, eat, sleep, and start all over again. The only thing that ever changed was the landscape. In her own time, of course, Kendra had known the lands under the Wizard Greeve's control to be desolate and decaying—and that's how she expected to find them here. And yet, with each step the army took towards Greeve's domain, the forests only seemed more lush and green, the rivers swelling their very banks.

And it wasn't right.

This Kendra knew, as sure as the braids on her head. *It's part of Greeve's trickery,* she told herself.

Six weeks after they had set off from the Lands of Een, the army arrived at Greeve's Green. Before them lay a carpet of emerald-green grass sprinkled with white and yellow flowers, sloping gently up towards a magnificent white palace. Each towering spire looked as if it had been built from a single sparkling stone, shimmering against the azure sky. Bedazzled, the Eens rubbed their eyes and gasped.

It was truly a place of wonder and beauty—but Kendra's stomach reeled with a terrible, sick feeling. "Now what do we do?" she asked Thunger.

"We make camp," he replied. "And wait for Greeve."

There was an extra buzz of activity among the army that afternoon. No one complained about thin rations or sore feet; all anyone could talk about was the white palace. "Can we live here?" Kendra heard more than one Een ask.

She could only shake her head in dismay. Other than herself, it seemed everyone—even the brothers—was under a spell.

Then, just as the sun was beginning to set, a tall figure robed in white appeared at the top of the slope, in front of the

gates of the palace. In one hand he clenched a long, crystal-white staff; the other hand was raised, palm open, to the sky.

"Brother Greeve," Thunger murmured in awe.

He gestured for Kendra to follow him to the head of the army, where the other brothers had assembled. There at last were Oki and Gayla, chaperoned by their guardian wizards. Kendra would have charged forward to embrace them, but Thunger put his heavy hand on her shoulder, and she didn't dare budge. Now all eyes turned to the white wizard standing at the palace gates. Everyone watched. Then, just as the sinking sun enveloped the Wizard Greeve in a blaze of light, a giant moth fluttered from his hand and crossed the plain. It delivered a scroll at Drake Dragonclaw's feet and buzzed back to its master.

"It is an invitation to dinner," the brother with the tousled hair said after reading the parchment. "Every Een must come. Even the soldiers and the helpers. All are to feast at the table of our brother."

"No!" Kendra cried. "Don't do it."

Every brother turned to gaze at her.

"Kendra!" Oki squealed. "B-be careful. The timel—,"

"It's a trap," Kendra declared. She knew Oki was worried about the fabric of time, about disrupting the future. But how could she think of such things? This wasn't a story in a book anymore. Standing behind her were a hundred and fifty Eens—real, living Eens—and they were about to go to their doom.

Thunger lowered himself to one knee and looked solemnly at Kendra. "These past weeks I have watched you, child. Not once have you stepped out of line, nor betrayed my confidence."

"Then you believe me?" Kendra asked.

"I believe that you *think* this is a trap," Thunger answered. "But I do not see this trap. I see a world of wonder, a palace of peace."

"It's a trick," Kendra urged.

"Listen, child," Izzen said. "We shall go and dine with our brother. And if it is a trap, we are six wizards to one, with an entire army at our command. He cannot harm us, even if he wishes."

"You don't understand," Kendra persisted. "His magic is strong—,"

Izzen raised his hand and Kendra's words caught in her throat. The matter had been settled.

If the outside of the palace had seemed magnificent, then the inside was even more so. If you had seen it, then you might have been reminded of a Romanesque castle, for the palace had high, arched ceilings, recessed galleries, and tall, austere doorways. Yet, unlike most castles, this place was not built of ordinary gray stone, but of pure white marble.

It took them some time to follow the Wizard Greeve through the corridors. *It's like a maze,* Kendra thought with a shudder. By the time everyone was assembled in the opulent banquet hall the sky had reached full dark, with a round moon glowering down from a window above.

In the very center of the hall was a crystal-white cauldron on a pedestal. Around it, arranged in radiating circles, were curved, white tables to seat the large assemblage. And now, amidst this lavish splendor, there came swirling from the cauldron the most intoxicating and tantalizing aromas. Even Kendra, despite her apprehension, felt her nose twitch at the redolent smells.

Everyone was seated, with the six wizard brothers guided to the innermost circle of tables, closest to the cauldron. Kendra, Oki, Gayla, and Clovin sat at the next ring, right behind Leemus.

It was the first time Kendra had been able to talk to her companions in weeks. Frantically, she whispered, "We have to get out of here."

"Yeah, I missed you, too," Gayla retorted. "How about a 'Hello' or 'How have you been for the last six weeks?'"

"How about we're all going to die if we stay here?" Kendra snapped.

"Oh, don't think of eggs!" Oki mumbled, and Clovin added a chatter for good measure.

"Are you sure you're not wrong about everything?" Gayla asked Kendra. "I mean, look at this place. It's amazing. Maybe the history books got it wrong."

Grendel Greeve took to the pedestal and, in his hooded white robe, almost seemed to glow. Standing tall and magnificent, he raised his staff and proclaimed, "Welcome, Brothers, welcome all, to my domain. For many moons you have journeyed the wilds of the world, far from your homes and loved ones. But now your travails shall receive just reward. Now you shall know what is coming to you."

With these words said, he lowered his staff into the great cauldron and began to stir—vigorously—and as he did, what had been a pleasant, delicious aroma began to turn sharp and bitter. It was as if the room started to spin (Kendra clutched the table to steady herself) and the white all around them began to evaporate, like sheets of paint peeling from the walls, revealing rough gray stones. The cauldron had changed too, from dazzling white to rock as black as death, and now the Wizard Greeve—his own robe having shimmered to the color of midnight—stirred his pot like a creature possessed, his eyes glowing fierce red and a chortle cackling in his throat.

There was a louder sound, though. It came from the cauldron itself, a high-pitched wail that grew in intensity, like the sound of a teakettle coming to a boil.

"Y-you're right, Braids!" Gayla cried over the shriek. "We have to get out of here!"

Kendra looked desperately at the Een army and then at the rest of the elders. They were all frozen, as if in some sort of trance. But not Kendra. She could feel her tell-tale spark flaring inside her, the one that always told her to take action. If there was ever a moment to trust her instincts, it was now. Quickly, she scurried under the table, which was beginning to show its true form: a crude block of stone supported by two pillars.

"I said we have to leave, not hide!" Gayla yelled.

"What we have to do is save Leemus!" Kendra called over her shoulder.

She crawled out from under the other side of the

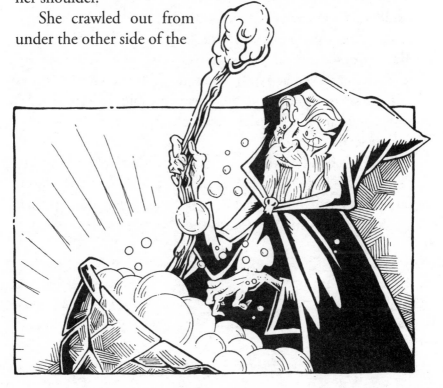

table and, with a wave of her wand, yanked Leemus's chair so that he tumbled backwards with a crash. Another motion of her wand pulled him across the floor and under the table to where Oki, Gayla, and Clovin were anxiously staring at the cauldron.

Kendra looked at it, too. The sinister stone urn was beginning to splinter and crack, and through these fissures she could see its contents glowing angry and hot. The whole cauldron was swelling, like a balloon. The shriek grew to a painful, unbearable whine. At any moment Kendra knew the black kettle would burst and cast its dreadful curse.

"Quickly—flip the table!" Kendra shouted at Gayla.

Together they raised their wands and turned the table on its side with a heavy thud. They ducked and took cover—just as the cauldron shattered in an explosion of burning light. The curse, like a vicious and frenzied creature escaping from its cage, screeched across the banquet hall. Kendra felt claws of light smash against the table; even though it was made of stone, it trembled from the impact. Panic-stricken, Kendra squeezed her eyes shut.

Only seconds later, the hall had fallen into complete silence. Kendra opened her eyes, rose to her feet, and—even though she had known all along what would happen—gasped.

They were completely surrounded by monsters.

CHAPTER 25

The
End
of the Days
Een
of

Ungers, Goojuns,
Orrids, Izzards, Krakes—it
was like being in the middle
of a nightmarish sea of claws
and fangs, fists and tails.
With a quiver, Kendra realized that each brother who
had been struck by the curse
had been transformed into a
separate creature, and his regiment
along with him. Now she watched,
frozen in horrific shock, as these
monsters of Een began to stretch
and groan, finding life in their new
and disfigured forms.

The Wizard Greeve was still on
his pedestal, straddling the now-shat-
tered remains of his urn. He seemed more
savage and wild than the creatures he had
just created.

"Go forth, Brothers!" he screeched, his eyes still burning
red. "Seek the Lands of Een! Hunt its pathetic people and
bring them before me. We shall cast them through my door of

doom, and they will be Eens no more! Together we shall bring the Days of Een to an end!"

A jubilant chorus of grunts and groans came from the throng of monsters. If they remembered that they had been Eens, they seemed not to care.

Greeve tilted back his head and cackled so loudly that the whole dark hall echoed with the sound. Then he pointed a long and crooked finger at Kendra and proclaimed, "Let the hunting begin."

Every beady eye in that wretched room now turned towards her. At her feet, Oki was trembling uncontrollably and Gayla was sitting against the overturned table with a look in her eyes that Kendra couldn't decipher. It was like she was in another world. Then Clovin chattered, and Leemus sprang to alertness, his own trance broken. He rose to his feet, tall and mighty, staff clenched determinedly in one hand.

Kendra saw Greeve's eyes flash with momentary fear. Leemus murmured a spell, at the same time bringing his staff against the floor with such a tremendous thump that the whole chamber rattled. And then—for just a moment—every creature around them seemed to freeze.

"RUN!" Leemus boomed.

With a chatter, Clovin led the way, bounding across the chamber and scurrying through the swarm of crooked limbs. At first, Gayla didn't budge. Kendra clutched her by the hand and pulled her after Clovin. Oki came next, and Leemus took up the rear. They had just reached the entrance to the banquet hall when the freeze spell snapped and the monsters sprang to life. Leemus slammed the two mighty doors behind them with a wave of his staff and cast a locking spell.

"It won't hold them long," he announced.

They raced through the palace—which, of course, was a palace no more, but the dark and dismal temple maze of the Wizard Greeve. Between them and escape was a jumble of twisting passages, dead-end corridors, and false leads; but with quickness of foot and sureness of direction, Clovin led them through each and every turn. Not once did he make a mistake—as Oki explained afterwards, the squirrel was in many ways still wild, and he followed every instinct to lead them towards safety.

Behind them, Kendra could hear the doors of the banquet hall burst open and the sounds of the monsters as they surged through the maze, roaring, growling, squawking.

Then Kendra saw the front gate of the temple, though now it looked very different from the one they had entered earlier that night. She could tell, even from the inside, that it was the Door to Unger. Its mouth—a set of wooden planks that looked like a row of teeth—now began to shut, just as the haunting sound of the Wizard Greeve's cackle emanated from the heart of his wretched temple.

Clovin dashed through the closing Door, Kendra stumbling behind, desperately yanking Gayla along with her. She felt a *whoosh of wind* past one ear, and out of the corner of her eye saw a long spear rattle off the stones in front of her. The very weapons that had been fashioned to protect Eens were now being used against them.

Once past the Door, Kendra turned and saw Leemus flick his long staff at the onslaught of spears, rocks, and other weapons—instantly, the deadly projectiles were transformed into a harmless shower of cherry blossoms that fluttered lightly to the ground. Then, urging Oki through the Door with one hand, the old wizard bustled through himself, just as the great teeth slammed shut with the sound of grinding stone and splintering wood.

Kendra looked up at the monstrous stone face that was the Door to the maze.

No one will ever walk out that way again, Kendra thought. *How many Eens will be tossed through this terrible Door over the next two thousand years? How many will know Greeve's curse?*

She was still holding Gayla's hand, and now she looked up at the bewildered Teenling, the girl who would one day be her mother. *My brother's going to go through there,* Kendra thought. *And maybe my father, and you . . .*

She couldn't bear the thought of it.

"Come," Leemus urged. "We must make haste."

It was still night, but in the moonlight Kendra could see that the plain before them was no longer one of grass and flowers, but rather a stretch of desolate rock. Across this they raced, desperate to put as much distance as they could between them and the temple.

At last, Leemus brought them to a stop. They were all panting, even the wizard. He sat cross-legged on the rocks and closed his eyes.

"This is no time to meditate!" Kendra cried. "They're coming after us. And if they take us back through the Door, we'll all be—,"

"Hush now," Leemus said in a stern but calm voice. "If I am to save us—and all of Een—I need you to be silent."

Kendra clutched Gayla's hand and watched the wizard. He placed his staff on the rocks in front of him, raised his hands to the air, and began to hoot. It would have sounded comical if the situation had not been so grave.

Moments later, Kendra heard another hoot, this one coming from the skies. She looked up to see five dark shapes fluttering against the light of the moon. Owls! With a rustle of

feathers, the magnificent birds landed alongside them. Without even opening his eyes, Leemus rose to his feet and placed his hand upon the soft, white head of the largest bird.

The owl made a clucking noise; something seemed to pass between the wizard and the majestic bird. Kendra plucked anxiously at a braid; she could hear the rumble of Greeve's creatures, and knew that the Door to Unger had opened once again to let them pass through and continue the chase. At any moment they would be swarmed by the ferocious army.

At last, Leemus opened his eyes and turned to Kendra and the others. "This is Prospero, King of Owls. Do not fear him, my friends; for while his beak is fierce, his heart is as gentle as a feather. He will deliver us from this wretched domain."

No one argued with the wizard's proposition; indeed, the owls did not seem half so savage as the creatures they could all hear in the distance. Quickly, they each scrambled onto the back of an owl, and the regal birds took to the indigo skies. As they ascended, the roar of the monsters grew dim. Kendra looked down at the Greeven Wastes and, with a sigh of relief, watched its dark expanse melt into the night.

Straight as arrows, the owls flew. How many hours passed, Kendra could not be sure.

Was that what Leemus thought we were meant to do? Kendra wondered, her mind reeling. *To save him from the curse?*

Then there was Gayla. Kendra just couldn't shake that look she had seen in her mother's eyes. Something had seized hold of her the moment she had witnessed the curse of Greeve—and it gave Kendra a chill.

Kendra awoke with a start and realized that her owl had come to a landing. She climbed down and rubbed her eyes; she must have nodded off sometime during the night. The sun was just beginning to break over the horizon, and standing in front of them was the twisted tree that served as the home of Leemus Longshanks. The old wizard scratched each owl on its feathery head, thanked them with a hoot, and sent them off to find their rest.

Kendra stared at the wizard. If Gayla had changed, then so had he. His face was sunken and stained with tears. And there was something else as well: over the course of their flight, Leemus had plaited his long shanks of hair into four braids.

"I wear them in your honor," the old wizard told Kendra. "You acted as my Eengels, just as the stars foretold." The old wizard then turned and gazed intently upon Clovin. Leemus bowed before the squirrel, then pronounced, "As for you, my fine furry friend, you too have proven your worth in the dark temple. As such, I hereby declare you Captain of Een, protector of all within this land. May you serve it well, with all the grace and dignity of our people." After a pause, Leemus smiled and said, "And now, my cosmic travelers, sleep awaits you in the house. Go find your dreams—you have earned them."

"Won't you rest, Elder Longshanks?" Kendra asked.

"That name is now a stranger to me," Leemus said. "I shall go evermore by Leemus Longbraids, the name you gave me. And I cannot rest, kind Eengel—for even though I might, the enemies of Een will not. Hunt us they will, until every last Een has been cast into that dark maze and perverted into a creature of claw and fang."

"It's the end of Een," Gayla mumbled, looking dazed and overwhelmed.

"Fret not the future," Leemus told her. "Nor pine for the past. Een will be saved yet."

"What are you going to do?" Oki asked.

"I shall build a wall," Leemus declared. "One that will protect Een from the outside world, one that cannot be battered or broken."

"One that can't even be seen," Kendra murmured.

"Why, yes," Leemus said. "An invisible curtain of magic."

CHAPTER 26

Kendra Puts a Fold in the Fabric of Time

Now you know, dear reader, how the Land of Een came to be. You know why the Eens wear braids, why they built the curtain, even why they turned into such a fretful and frightened people. If you find it a lot to ponder, then you can only imagine the thoughts whirling through Kendra's mind.

Eventually our young heroine slept, but not long and not well. Perhaps you have had those nights; no matter how exhausted you might be, your slumber offers you no rest. For Kendra, it was a sleep plagued by a nightmare, the same one, over and over again. In it, she was standing at the edge of Een, watching her mother walk away into the distance, only to be suddenly devoured by a ferocious Unger. It was a dream Kendra had had many times. But this time it was different. This time her mother was the fifteen-year-old Gayla. This time her mother was someone she actually *knew*.

At last she awoke and sat up. They were all sharing one large bed, and—to Kendra's surprise—Gayla was also awake. The feisty Teenling was staring at the wall, that strange fire in her eyes.

"They're . . . they're Goojuns and Ungers and . . . everything," Gayla said. "It changes *everything*. All this time, it's been us against them. But they *are* us. Krimson always said he thought there was a connection. I used to tell him to shut up and stop playing fairy tale. But he was right. He was *right*." She gave her head a shake and looked directly at Kendra. "I've got to get back; I've got to tell him. I've got to set everyone right."

"What if they don't believe you?" Kendra asked. "And what about your brother? And about marrying Burdock?"

"That . . . that doesn't matter any more," Gayla said. "It seems such a small problem now. Don't you get it? The world is so much bigger than us, Braids. And there's got to be a way to make it right."

Kendra suddenly realized what that look was in Gayla's eyes. It was obsession. Gayla had witnessed firsthand the curse of Greeve and it had galvanized her, transformed her into the very person Kendra had always heard about: the loud, outspoken sorceress with the "strange" ideas about the history of Een.

And she will fight with the elders of Een, Kendra thought. *She will try to convince them of the truth. But no one will believe her—not even Uncle Griffinskitch. And then one day she'll leave Een and . . .*

Kendra felt a sob welling in her throat.

I'll be alone.

"I . . . I have to get some air," Kendra told Gayla.

She scrambled out of bed and wandered down into the kitchen. She was grateful to find the house empty and quiet, and she sat at the table and rested her head against the rough wooden surface.

How can I let her go? Kendra asked herself.

Then she noticed at her elbow a bottle of Eenberry ink, a feather pen, and a roll of parchment. It was as if they had been set there purposely for her. Before she knew it, the pen was in her hand and she was scrawling out a letter. For an hour she wrote, thoughts and feelings pouring onto the parchment until at last, exhausted, she fell asleep, cheek against the drying ink.

When she awoke, it was to a rough jostle from Gayla. "Come on, Braids."

Kendra's eyes flickered open. She slowly lifted her head to see Gayla and Oki staring at her.

"You have ink on your face," Gayla told her. "What's that you've been writing?"

Kendra looked down at the parchment. "Oh, nothing," she said, quickly folding the note and sticking it in a pocket.

"It's time to go home," Gayla announced. "Back to where we belong. Me to my time, you to yours."

"Shouldn't we wait to say good-bye to Elder Longbraids?" Oki asked.

"He'll expect us to be gone," Gayla said with a sort of smile. "We are Eengels after all. It's in our nature to mysteriously disappear."

"Oki and I need to get back to the Forests of Wretch before we jump," Kendra said, thinking of her friends on the cloud ship. "That's where we started from. That's where my master will be looking for us."

"I'll make sure you get there safely," Gayla assured her.

It was a quiet walk through the forest. So much had happened that no one really knew what to say—especially Kendra. All she could think about was that she was about to be separated from her mother, and she had no idea if she would ever see her again.

After a few hours, Gayla brought them to a halt. "I think this is the right place," she said. "One day this place will be the Forests of Wretch, crawling with Goojuns."

"Where's the tree we landed in?" Kendra asked.

"It's not here yet," Gayla said. "It'll be hundreds of years before it even takes seed. But don't worry—it's close enough to the right place. We can jump from here."

Kendra pulled out the Kazah Stone and passed it to Gayla. "I guess you better be the one to lead us," Kendra said. "It's your time we're going to, after all. You can imagine it best."

Gayla nodded and held the ring carefully in her palm. "Grab hold," she said, just before closing her eyes.

A few minutes later, they were sitting in the shadows of the forest.

"We're back in my time," Gayla said confidently as she passed Kazah back to Kendra. "Look, there's the tree you first fell into. The branches are still freshly snapped."

"I guess this is good-bye then," Kendra said. For a moment she just stared at Gayla.

"Come on, Braids," Gayla said. "I'm assuming you want to hug me or some other nonsense."

Kendra nodded and rushed forward to throw herself into Gayla's arms. Part of her wished she could just stay in this time with her mother, forever. In one corner of her mind she could hear the warning of her older self, the blind sorceress: *Start pulling at the tapestry of time, and everything you know just may unravel.* But in that instant Kendra didn't care. *I deserve a mother,* she thought. Then she remembered the letter she had written the night before. Sneakily, Kendra pulled it from her robe and tucked it into one of Gayla's pockets.

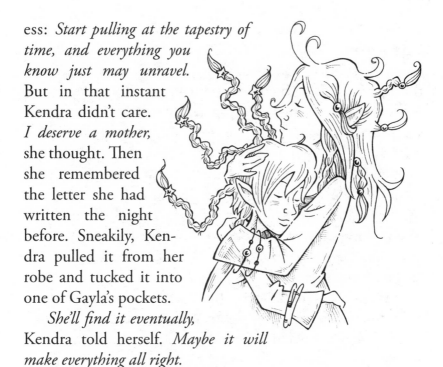

She'll find it eventually, Kendra told herself. *Maybe it will make everything all right.*

Then they heard a distant voice call, "GAYLA!"

"That's Beards," Gayla said in surprise. "I guess he figured out I'm not in the Elder Stone anymore."

Kendra had to think for a moment; it seemed like a lifetime ago since Gayla's trial.

"Probably in a heap of trouble," Gayla added.

"He sounds more worried than angry, if you ask me," Kendra said.

"Hmph," Gayla grunted. "Well, I guess I'd better go. You two can jump once I get Beards out of here. You know what, Braids? Well . . . If I did have a sister, I guess I'd want her to be you. Even though you are annoying." She flashed Kendra a smile, then looked over at Oki and said, "Well, Eeks, any final words?"

"Knowing you was one big *floofenflah*," Oki replied, giving her a hug.

"I'll assume that's a compliment," Gayla said, scratching the top of his head. Then, with a final wave, she walked away.

As soon as she was out of sight, Oki turned to Kendra. "I saw you sneak that scrap of parchment into her pocket. What was it?"

Kendra shook her head. "Just . . . just a good-bye note. Come on. Time for us to go." She paused and gazed down at the Kazah Stone. "The crack is even wider now," she said. "It's a good thing this is our last jump."

"Thank eggs for that," Oki announced. "I've had enough of time travel."

"Me too," Kendra said. "But I guess we accomplished everything we needed to, right? We rescued Uncle Griffinskitch. We rescued Elder Longbraids. Now everything's as it should be."

But, as she was about to find out, she couldn't have been more wrong.

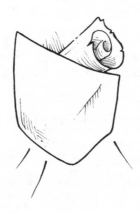

CHAPTER 27

How Everything Changed in the Land of Een

Even the most steadfast of adventurers eventually longs for home. For Kendra, home currently meant the cloud ship where she could reunite with Uncle Griffinskitch and her friends Ratchet, Jinx, and Professor Bumblebean. It was these friends that filled her concentration as she clutched the Kazah Stone. She imagined them, standing there amidst the swirling snows of winter, waiting for her and Oki.

In a flash, the Kazah Stone performed its magic. Kendra felt a sudden chill around her ankles. This was to be expected—she was bound to end up knee-deep in snow. What she didn't expect was to open her eyes and be confronted by a black-bearded dwarf looming over her with a mischievous smirk, a club in one hand and a net in the other.

"EEK!" Oki squealed.

The little mouse tugged at Kendra, and she rolled over just as the dwarf swung the club. It crashed to the ground in an explosion of snow.

Kendra scrambled to her feet and fled after Oki. Even as they dashed across the snow, Kendra could see countless more dwarves storming through the woods, all armed with nets and weapons. Eens were scampering everywhere and the vale echoed with their screams.

What in the world is going on? Kendra thought.

The dwarf with the black beard was hot on her heels—she could hear and smell him. Kendra desperately yanked her wand from her belt, turned, and sent a blast of lightning at the foul pursuer. Her bolt struck him right in the beard, causing him to stumble back and holler (though more in surprise than pain, Kendra guessed). She knew it wouldn't slow him down for long.

Suddenly, a hole opened in the snowy ground right in front of them, and there appeared the familiar face of Juniper Jinx.

"Quickly!" the tiny grasshopper hollered. "This way."

They stumbled forward into the hole, which Kendra now realized was capped with a lid disguised to look like a rock. As soon as they were through, Jinx quickly shut the lid. They found themselves inside a small tunnel lit only by a dim lantern.

"We thought you were dead!" Jinx exclaimed, bounding forward to enfold Kendra and Oki in her arms.

"Uh . . . Jinx, are you okay?" Kendra panted. "You're not exactly the hugging type."

"Yeah," Oki added, squirming free of the grasshopper's four-armed embrace. "You're more of the punching and kicking type."

"What are you talking about?" Jinx asked. "I've never punched a soul in my life! And, oh—please do call me Juniper. Even in times like these, it's so barbaric to call someone by her last name."

Kendra looked at Oki in complete puzzlement. They had *always* called Jinx by her last name. "Sure," Kendra said, skeptically tugging a braid. "What in the name of Een is going on? Where did all those dwarves come from?"

"Come on, let's get somewhere safer—and warmer," Jinx said as she led them down the dark tunnel. "And you know those dwarves. They're Ratbaggio's thugs. They've been prowling around here for the last couple of days."

"Ratbaggio?" Oki asked.

"He's the ringmaster of that cruel carnival show; but you know that—are you two sure *you're* okay?" Jinx asked, pausing to look at them in concern.

"Kendra," Oki whimpered. "Something's wrong. Very, very wrong."

"Oh, don't fret," Jinx said, hugging Oki again. "Let's get below where it's warmer. I doubt there's much Eencake left, but I'm sure Master Bumblebean can prepare some tea."

"Did you just call Bumblebean your master?" Kendra asked.

"Of course!" Jinx said. "But it's *Professor* Bumblebean to you, Kendra. You should try and show respect to one of the most distinguished and learned Eens in all the world!"

Kendra didn't know what to say. She just tugged one of her braids.

They eventually arrived at a small alcove where they saw Professor Bumblebean and Ratchet. Both looked like they had been through harsh times, for their clothes were patched and threadbare, and even the Professor's spectacles were cracked. The small room mirrored their condition. It was sparsely furnished with only a few simple comforts.

"Happy days!" Professor Bumblebean cheered upon seeing Kendra and Oki. "You found them, dear Juniper! Good work!"

"Oh, my pleasure," Jinx blushed, batting her long-lashed eyes at him.

"There's the apprentice I've been looking for," Ratchet said, tousling the top of Oki's head. "I was certain you had perished. What happened?"

"We could ask you the same thing," Kendra remarked. "We have no idea what's going on. The last thing we remember is falling from the cloud ship."

"Cloud ship?" Ratchet asked. "Whatever is that?"

"The *Big Bang!*" Oki cried. "You know, the flying ship we built!? It's . . . it's, well, you know—splendulous!"

"I'm certain I don't know what you're talking about," Ratchet admitted, scratching his chin. "But you should employ sensible, real words, Oki. Don't you want our inventions to be taken seriously?"

"Eek!" Oki cried. "What's happened to all of you?"

"Don't worry, little one," Jinx told the mouse, squeezing him tight. "Oh, you're so cute, I could hug you all day."

200

"You need to tell us what's going on," Kendra insisted. "Why are you living in this hole? And why are the Eens all running around the Forests of Wretch? Why aren't they hiding behind the magic curtain?"

"The magic curtain!" Professor Bumblebean exclaimed in surprise. "Come, Kendra, you know the magic curtain fell over a year ago!"

"It fell?!" Kendra gasped. "But what about Faun's End? And the Elder Stone? And—,"

"All obliterated," Ratchet answered. "Since then, it's been every Een for himself, hiding under stump and stone from the truculent beasts of the outside world. But if the professor and I have anything to do about it, we will raise the curtain again."

"Master Bumblebean thinks he's discovered a new and improved magic formula," Jinx gushed. "Isn't he absolutely superb? He's handsome *and* intelligent!"

"Oh, don't think of eggs!" Oki groaned, throwing himself against the ground and clutching his head.

"You know, I think you two have been through too much lately," stated Professor Bumblebean. "Juniper, why not take them down to the side chamber for some rest?"

"Certainly," Jinx chimed. With two of her four arms, she grabbed Kendra and Oki and led them down a tunnel until they came to an even smaller hole carved out of the cold earth.

"Wait a minute," Kendra said as the grasshopper was about to leave. "Where's Uncle Griffinskitch?"

Jinx looked at her with her large insect eyes. "Oh, Kendra," she said after a moment. "You really should lie down. I'll bring you some tea in a moment."

"I don't want tea!" Kendra cried. "I want to know where my uncle is!"

"I'll be back in a moment," Jinx said, hurriedly turning and bounding down the tunnel.

Kendra whirled and looked at Oki. "What in the name of all things Een is going on?" she demanded.

"I've been trying to figure it out," Oki said, nervously rubbing his paws together. "I think we changed the timeline

somehow, Kendra. Something we did in the past has completely changed our present. Jinx is kind, Ratchet is serious, and Professor Bumblebean doesn't even use big words!"

Kendra sat down, her mind flooding with worry. "And the whole Land of Een has been destroyed," she added.

"We have to go back," Oki said. "We have to change whatever we did. But what was it?"

"It . . . it was *me*," Kendra murmured after a moment. "It's what I did."

"What was that?" Oki asked anxiously.

"That note I slipped into Gayla's pocket," Kendra explained. "I told her . . . "

"Oh no!" Oki squealed. "Don't tell me you—,"

"I did," Kendra admitted. "I told her I was her daughter. I told her that she was going to become so consumed with proving to the council that we were actually the same as Ungers and the rest that she would one day run away from Een, and that I would be orphaned. I *begged* her not to leave Een."

"EEK!" Oki screamed. "Kendra, how could you? That was it! That's changed everything! Your mother never ended up fighting the council. She never left Een. Your brother never became Trooogul. That means . . . that means . . . that means a *tribbillionous* things have changed that shouldn't have!"

"How was I supposed to know all this would happen?" Kendra cried frantically. "I just thought I could have a mother. Did you see how obsessed she was? She cared more about that curse than anything else."

"But she's supposed to!" Oki wailed.

"I thought I could make everything better. But it's much, much worse."

"We've got to go back," Oki said. "We need to fix it. Right now. We've got to sneak that letter *out* of Gayla's pocket."

Kendra didn't argue. She pulled out the Kazah Stone and slid it onto her finger. She closed her eyes and tried to concentrate—but she couldn't. There was a loud series of thuds coming from above.

"What is that?" Kendra asked, opening her eyes.

Suddenly, the point of a pickaxe came slicing through the ceiling, sending down a shower of rocks and snow. Kendra and Oki both screamed as a giant hole appeared in the ceiling and there, glaring at them, was the dwarf they had just recently escaped. This time, he had help.

"Looksee here, I found their nest!" the dwarf chortled to his fellow. "Ol' Ratbag is goin' to grin ear to ear."

With a squeal, Oki made an attempt to scurry down the tunnel, but the dwarf with the black beard nabbed him by the tail, plucked him out of the hole, and stuffed him into his sack. Kendra reached for her wand, but it was too late. The second dwarf had his greasy hands around her braids and with cruel force yanked her upwards. He snatched away her wand and, dangling her upside down, began to shake her. Out came the Kazah Stone, into his waiting hand.

"Oooh, shiny!" he tittered, and then he dumped Kendra into his own sack.

"Oki!" Kendra screamed—but all she heard was a muffled reply. The mouse was already being taken away by the other dwarf, and now Kendra felt her own sack bounce atop her captor's back.

Where's he taking me? Kendra wondered desperately.

This question was answered only a few minutes later, when she heard the clang of a door and was unceremoniously dumped onto a hard, cold wooden platform. She rubbed her eyes and turned to see the dwarf smiling smugly through a row of iron bars.

She was in some sort of cage. It was filthy and, despite the frigid temperature, slick with slop and slime, so putrid in stench it made her gag. Looking past the dwarf, Kendra could see a whole caravan of cages, each of them on wheels and arranged in a circle. Each carriage seemed to hold a different creature; Kendra could see not only Eens, but gryphons, fauns, and even a mermaid (she was in a tank frosted with a thin crust of ice).

It's the carnival that Jinx was talking about, Kendra thought.

"Ratbag will be all too happy to add this shiny trinket to his treasures," the dwarf snickered, holding out his greasy palm to reveal the Kazah Stone. "Me bets there's extra ale for me tonight!" Then, whistling a happy tune, the vile fellow turned and waddled away.

"Oki, where are you?" Kendra moaned.

"K-Kendra?" came a voice—but it wasn't Oki.

Kendra whirled around and gazed into the dark recesses of the cage. "Wh-who's there?" Kendra stammered, clutching anxiously at her braids. The voice sounded familiar, almost like . . .

Then a figure staggered out of the shadows, into the meager winter light, and Kendra cried out in shock.

It was her mother. And she was so very old.

CHAPTER 28

The
Dream
that
Died

Gayla Griffinskitch
changed—a lot. Gone was
her wild, unfettered hair
adorned with beads and
baubles. Gone was her
loose-fitting robe hang-
ing off one shoulder.
Now her hair was more
gray than brown, tied
in two simple plaits. It
was her eyes, however,
that had changed the
most. Once full of fire,
now they were dull and dim
and sagging with the weight of so
many wrinkles.

Of course, to a certain extent,
Gayla was supposed to look this way. She
was exactly the right age for this present time, for
we must remember that Kendra and Oki had jumped ahead
almost thirty-five years after saying their farewells to the Teenling Gayla. Still, it spooked Kendra and she just stood there,
as stiff and frozen as the iron bars that imprisoned them.

But her mother showed no such hesitation. She rushed forward and reeled Kendra into her arms. "Thank the ancients," she exclaimed, kissing the side of Kendra's head. "I thought you were dead."

Her hands were so ice-cold that it sent a shiver down Kendra's spine; she couldn't help but to pull away. "Why does everyone keep saying that?" Kendra asked.

Her mother gazed into her eyes. "The Goojuns," she replied. "They snatched you and Oki almost two months ago. How did you escape?"

Kendra fussed with a braid. "W-we didn't," she stammered. "It wasn't us. I mean, I guess it was us . . . but not *us*."

"What are you talking about?"

Kendra didn't even know where to begin. She turned and stared through the prison bars at the rest of the caravan. She could hear the whines and moans of the captives, punctuated here and there by the cruel crack of a dwarf's whip.

It's a nightmare, Kendra thought. Then out loud she said, "Gayla?"

"Gayla?" her mother echoed in surprise. "That's a name I haven't heard in a long, long time. Since before you were born. What makes you call me that? I've always been 'momma' to you."

"Always?" Kendra asked, looking back at her mother.

"Since you were little."

Of course, Kendra thought. *This is my mother after marrying my father and becoming Kayla Kandlestar. And if she never left Een, then I grew up knowing her. She . . . she truly is my mother in this timeline.*

It was almost too much for Kendra to bear. But there was something not quite right, she realized, as she gazed into her mother's face. It was her eyes. They were so dull, so . . . lifeless.

That doesn't come from just growing old, Kendra said to herself. *Winter Woodsong is over a hundred years old, and her eyes still sparkle like the stars.*

"Do you remember me?" Kendra asked.

"Why, of course, Kendra! It's only been two months."

"That's not what I mean," Kendra said. "I mean from when *you* were young. From when Oki and I . . . "

"Fell through the crack in Kazah and landed in my time," Kayla finished. "Yes. I remember it. So that's happened now, has it, from your perspective?"

Kendra nodded. "So you remember going to the Days of Een? You remember the letter I wrote you?"

"Yes, I cherish it. It saved our family. For a while at least."

"What do you mean?" Kendra asked, anxiously tugging on a braid. "Where are they?"

"Kiro and your father were captured by Ungers. Almost one year ago."

"And Uncle Griffinskitch?" Kendra could barely get the words out.

"Kendra, you know this. He died—,"

Kendra's hand flew to her mouth, trying to stifle a sob; but she couldn't help it. The tears were surging down her cheeks.

Kendra's mother pulled her tight, cradling her against her chest. "Kendra, what's going on? Tell me."

"I'm not . . . I'm not your Kendra, not really," Kendra tried to explain through her tears. "I'm the Kendra that came to visit you when you were fifteen. But when I jumped back to my own time, I ended up here."

"This *is* your time, Kendra," Kayla said.

"No, it isn't!" Kendra cried. "This isn't the way it's supposed to be. It's not right. In *my* time, where I jumped from, Uncle Griffinskitch is still alive, the curtain's still there . . . "

Kayla looked at Kendra intently. "Are you telling me there's a life different from this one? One where the magic curtain yet stands? One filled with . . . hope?" Her eyes flickered; for a moment Kendra thought she saw her fire.

Kendra nodded, wiping at her tears.

"We have *no* hope here," Kayla said quietly.

"But in the other time, it's not all . . . I mean, you . . ." Kendra couldn't finish her sentence.

"I'm gone," Kayla finished for her. "Along with your father and Kiro . . . just how you described it in that letter."

"And because I wrote it everything changed."

Kendra's mother looked at her steadily, then stooped to pick something from the corner of the cell. It was a tiny stuffed rabbit, faded and worn.

"What is that?" Kendra asked.

"It's . . . it's all I have left of you," Kayla replied. "I was holding it the day the dwarves captured me."

"I've never seen it before," Kendra said.

"I made it for you . . . when you were little," her mother explained. "I suppose what I mean to say is that I made it for the Kendra that I knew. I'm guessing that you, in your timeline, never had an Een doll."

"I grew up with Uncle Griffinskitch," Kendra said. "He wasn't much of a seamstress."

Kayla smiled sadly. "No, I suppose you're right." She stared down at the tiny ragdoll rabbit. "You know," she said, "I stuffed it with cotton from the cloudtail plant."

"What's that?" Kendra asked.

"It's an Een plant and very magical," Kayla explained.

"Why are you telling me all of this?" Kendra asked.

Kayla clutched the doll tight to her chest. "*My* Kendra is gone," she said. "Just as *your* mother is gone. My Kendra . . . I fear I shall never see her again. But where you came from, there's still hope for us, for our whole family. Isn't that right?"

Kendra nodded.

"Do you still have the ring?" her mother asked.

"The dwarves took it," Kendra said, fidgeting with a braid.

"We have to get it back," Kayla said. "Here, stop that tugging. How many times have I told you?"

Kendra looked at her blankly. "Never."

Kayla shook her head in confusion. "Of course . . . see, even I get confused. That's what I used to tell *my* Kendra. And now *you* are here. But you shouldn't be."

"Oki said we have to go back and steal back the letter before you read it," Kendra said.

"He's right," Kayla said, slowly nodding. "If I don't read that letter, then I'll end up leaving Een, just like you said."

"But then I won't have you!" Kendra exclaimed. "At least in this timeline you're here. You're safe."

"Kendra," her mother said softly. "Look around you. Our world is in shambles. Our entire family is gone."

"But you're here."

"Kendra, look at me. What do you see?"

Kendra gazed at her mother's face and shivered, but it wasn't just from the cold. Her mother's eyes were simply dead. Once they had been flaring with passion. But there was no trace of it now.

I see . . . I see a dream that's died, Kendra thought. But she didn't say it out loud. Instead she said, "I see my mother."

"Kendra," Kayla said, squeezing her close. "You have to do what is right for Een. Not just for me and you. Don't you see? The world is bigger than us."

CHAPTER 29

Ringmaster Ratbaggio's Cruel Circus

Be careful what you wish for. It's an expression we've all heard, and for Kendra it was never more true than now. She had finally found her adult mother, but it had come at a devastating cost. Her brother and father were still missing, Uncle Griffinskitch was dead, and the Land of Een was no more. As for her mother . . . well, Kayla Kandlestar was hardly a magnificent sorceress. Her spirit vanquished, she was a mere shell of the fiery fifteen-year-old girl who had witnessed firsthand the curse of the Wizard Greeve.

Little sleep came to Kendra that first night in the prison cart, but when she did finally drift off it was only to be rudely awoken early in the morning by the crack of a whip and a brutish song:

Freaks, freaks, beautiful freaks,
I love ta hear thar groans and eeks!
Claws, tails, horns, and beaks!
How I love me beautiful freaks!

Kendra gave her mother a startled glance and scrambled to the front of her cage to see a fat and vulgar figure strut into the circle of prison carts. He was a dwarf, but unlike his fellows, he was dressed in a garish coat trimmed with gold, a top hat, and a pair of dark boots. He might have looked glamorous if his costume had not been so tarnished and torn. Worst of all was his beard, for it was scraggly and red and crusted with scraps of food. In one grimy hand he carried a whip, which he cracked with malicious zeal at the bars of each cage as he passed.

Kendra rubbed her eyes. "It can't be . . . ," she thought aloud in disbelief.

She knew this dwarf—and if you have followed Kendra's adventures at all, then you know him, too. This was none other than Pugglemud, that raffish fiend who seemed to torment Kendra at every turn. He had been a treasure hunter, a king, a pirate—and now here he was, ringmaster of a terrible circus of atrocities. That was Pugglemud for you. He was like a tenacious weed; no matter how many times you plucked him, he kept coming back, each time stronger than the last.

When he arrived in front of Kendra, Pugglemud came to an abrupt halt. "Why, lemme have a look-see at yer hair," the dwarf proclaimed, scratching his beard to release a shower of moldy bread crumbs. "Yer a fine freak! I reckon ya be one of the new Een-weenies what my boys caught yesterday."

"Don't you know me, Pugglemud?" Kendra asked. "I know *your* foul stench—all too well."

The dwarf glared at her. Then, raising his whip, he warned, "I don't know how ya know that name, Eenee—but it ain't one I be goin' by these days. I be Ringmaster Ratbaggio and ya best be callin' me by it, don't ya know."

Kendra's mother scooted forward to pull Kendra away from the bars. "Excuse her insolence, Master Ratbaggio. She means no disrespect."

Kendra gave Kayla an incredulous look. This was definitely *not* the mother she had come to know. She glared back at Pugglemud. "Do you have my ring, *Master Ratbaggio?*" she asked in a sarcastic tone.

Pugglemud reached inside his cloak and pulled out the Kazah Stone. "This little shiny?" he grunted. "It's purty—though I like gold better. Tee hee!"

"Its cracked and useless," Kendra said, staring at the Stone with envy. "You should give it back to me."

"Jus' the fact ya want it means it's worth somethin'," Pugglemud tittered, tucking the Kazah Stone back in his coat. "So I'll be keepin' it anyhoo. Maybe I can sell it fer a gold coin or two. Tee hee!"

Then he turned and waddled off, cracking his whip in Kendra's direction for good measure.

"Kendra!" her mother hissed. "Watch your tongue; you'll get us both a lashing."

Kendra sighed and shook her head. She began to wonder if there was even a tiny part of Gayla Griffinskitch left in her mother.

The next few weeks were some of the most miserable of Kendra's life. The caravan was endlessly on the move, pulled by horse, mule, or—in some cases—magical creatures, like unicorns. The ride was rough, for the carts bounced and bumped over the frozen roads until Kendra's teeth rattled.

Still, these were the moments of relief, for it was when the caravan pulled into a town or settlement that the true horrors began. Pugglemud and his cronies would erect their tents and the prisoners were forced to perform for the amusement of the crowds. The unicorns jumped through hoops of fire, the mermaid somersaulted in her tank, and the Eens juggled balls and walked across tightropes suspended high above the ground. There were no safety nets, of course, and all the while Pugglemud cracked his whip. The crowds loved it. They came in abundant numbers to leer and gawk at the so-called freaks. Given the chance, they would poke and prod and even throw stones and rotten apples.

These performances were the only times Kendra had a chance to communicate with Oki; otherwise he was kept in a tiny birdcage in Pugglemud's personal sleeping carriage,

mostly because the fat ringmaster delighted in snapping him with his whip and hearing him squeal. It made Kendra's braids burn with rage; she spent many an hour desperately trying to hatch a plan of escape. But without her wand or the Kazah Stone, it all seemed so hopeless.

Whenever he could, Pugglemud would add new creatures to

his carnival. One day, when the caravan had camped for the evening, Kendra heard a clamorous scuffle and looked out of her prison cart to see that the dwarves had captured the most beautiful creature: the magnificent winged deer known as a peryton.

"I know him!" Kendra told her mother. "It's Prince!"

"Who?" Kayla asked, shuffling to the front of the cage.

"He's my friend," Kendra explained excitedly. "We've been through a lot together."

Yes, it was the prince of the perytons, the noble animal who had fought side by side with Kendra in that terrible gladiator arena known as the Rumble Pit. Together they had escaped to freedom—but that had been in Kendra's own time. In this timeline, the peryton was very much a prisoner, bound with ropes from the points of his magnificent antlers to the tips of his long white wings. Even so, the formidable beast fought his captors, pounding his heavy hooves against the snow and swinging his antlers. Pugglemud arrived on the scene, cursing and cracking his whip until they were able to tug the obstinate peryton into an empty cage right next to Kendra's. The last thing Pugglemud did before slamming the door on the peryton's cage was to pluck one of his glistening white feathers and stick it in his hat.

"Now that's a fancy-schmancy sight, Ratbaggio," one of Pugglemud's minions said, but the ringmaster's only response was to lash him with his whip.

"Prince!" Kendra called over to the giant winged deer, after the dwarves had disbanded to go about their carnival chores. "Are you okay?"

"Leave me be, underling," the peryton snorted. "I know you not."

"Yes, you do," Kendra insisted, craning her neck to see if she could catch a glimpse of the noble beast in the adjacent cart. And then, because Kendra knew it, she spoke the secret name that the peryton had once told her. A name is a very precious thing to the great winged creatures, and they tell them only to those they trust the most.

"Fur and feathers!" the peryton huffed in response. "What magic is this, that you can speak my name? I would pierce your tongue if my horns could reach you. Be gone, underling—and take your devilish sorcery with you!"

Kendra slunk back to the corner of her cage. A tear trickled down her cheek. *Everything in this time is completely wrong,* she thought. *Things just can't get much worse.*

But they could, of course—for, as Kendra was about to find out, the caravan was headed straight towards a place of almost certain doom: the Rumble Pit.

CHAPTER 30

S The Storm on the Seas of Ire

The Rumble Pit! Located in the belly of Krake Castle, it was a place of pain and misery, where many a creature from legend and lore had battled for survival. Why, you might ask? The answer is simple: to amuse Queen Krake and her legions of bird-like drones with the horrendous spectacle of the fight.

Kendra had never imagined she would have to return to that dreadful place—until the day Pugglemud gathered his thugs in front of the prison carts and announced: "Boys, we're goin' to be rollin' in gold—tee hee! Cuz I'm goin' ta sell the whole mess o' freaks to that queeny so she can put 'em to fightin' in her pit."

"Then what'll happen to the circus?" one of the dwarves asked.

"I'm shuttin' her down, don't ya know," Pugglemud retorted. "These freaks is becomin' more trouble than they're worth. And now I got me a peryton, rarest of all magic beasties. That queeny will pay through the beak fer him."

"You're a fool to go there," Kendra boldly interrupted from her prison cart. "You'll find only torment and torture in Krake Castle."

"And gold—tee hee!" Pugglemud sniggered, prancing over to spit at Kendra through the bars of her cage.

"You're mistaken," Kendra told him. "I've met this queen. She will snap your whip in two and toss you into the Rumble Pit along with the rest of us."

"Yer jus' trying to save yer own neck," Pugglemud scoffed, stroking the long peryton feather that adorned his hat. "Ya can bellyache all ya want, but it's of no account anyhoo—cuz you freaks is goin' to the Rumble Pit!"

He wandered off with a whistle and Kendra turned to stare glumly at her mother.

"You've been in this pit before?" Kayla asked.

Kendra nodded.

"How did you survive?"

"My friends," Kendra replied. "And Uncle Griffinskitch," she added forlornly. "But he's not coming to the rescue this time."

And so the caravan rolled across the countryside and eventually arrived in the port town of Ireshook, that wretched hive of gamblers, cheats, and sailors. Here Pugglemud bought passage on a large gnome ship to take them across the Seas of Ire to Krake Castle. The greedy dwarf booked a fancy cabin for himself and a few of his henchmen, but Kendra and the rest of the circus performers were left in their prison carts and loaded into the darkest and bottommost hold of the ship.

Now their situation seemed even more desperate than before. There was little light, the food was terrible, and the ship often rocked horribly. Kendra was constantly sick.

Then, one day, the ship began to pitch and roll more than usual. Even from the depths of the cargo hold, Kendra could hear the wail of the wind and the roar of the waves. She suddenly realized that they had been caught in a fierce storm and were at the mercy of the sea. The brakes had been set on the wheels of the prison carts to prevent them from rolling, but the ship tipped and tilted so dramatically that the cages began to slide across the floor of the cargo hold, smashing into each other along the way.

"Quickly, Kendra," Kayla gasped. "Brace yourself!"

Kendra wrapped both hands around an iron bar, but the whole cart now flew across the hold and slammed into the side of the ship with such force that she lost her grip and was pitched backwards, head over heels. It took a moment for her to collect her wits, and when she did, she realized the cage had burst open.

"Hurry," Kayla cried, yanking Kendra to her feet.

They scrambled out of the prison cart, and to her horror Kendra realized the cage wasn't the only thing broken. There was a huge fracture in the hull of the ship and seawater was gushing in.

We've struck rocks, Kendra thought. *We must be near shore.*

Some of the other prisoners were free, but many were still locked in their cages. They screamed for help; Kendra knew they would have no chance in the sinking ship. So, even as water swirled around her boots, she found a splintered timber and began using it to pry open cage doors or widen cracks that had already started in the sides of the carts.

I hope Oki's okay, she thought desperately—as far as she knew, he was still in his birdcage up in Pugglemud's personal quarters.

One of the unicorns was now free; with its mighty horn it began slashing open cages. The ship was listing sharply and water was up to Kendra's neck. She suddenly realized she had no idea where her mother was. Then the ship seemed to strike rocks again, for another part of the hull split and water roared *out* of the hold—and with it went Kendra.

These were some terribly anxious moments. The next thing Kendra knew, she was bobbing in the frigid waves beneath a dark sky. She paddled desperately. She saw silhouettes all about her, but had no strength to cry out to see if one of them was her mother. All her energy went to staying afloat.

Then, at long last, Kendra felt sand beneath her belly. She crawled forward until she could no longer feel the sea nipping at her feet. She tried to pull herself up, but her limbs felt like jelly, and at last she let exhaustion consume her, falling asleep beneath the tumultuous sky.

Kendra awoke to a squawking sound. Her eyes flickered open and she found herself surrounded by tall, imposing boulders. She remembered this rocky shore all too well; she looked up and, sure enough, saw the twisted towers of Krake Castle looming above. Somewhere inside that dark nest was the Rumble Pit—and it filled Kendra with dread.

She heard the squawking again and knew it couldn't be coming from the castle; it was too far away. She peered over the nearest boulder and, down the shoreline, spied the wreckage of the gnome ship. It had been ripped to shreds by the storm and lay in pieces on the shore, its timber carcass swarmed by a legion of Krake soldiers. Kendra could see the bird-like beasts plucking survivors from the ship's broken hull: dwarves, gnomes, Eens, and the other magical creatures. She could see a line of prisoners already being chained together. It was easy enough to make out the peryton, but she had to squint before seeing Oki and her mother there, too.

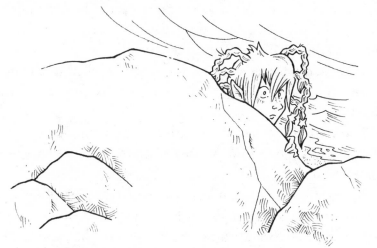

"At least they're alive," she thought aloud.

"Not fer long, I betcha."

Kendra looked down to see a pair of beady eyes glaring up at her over a long sharp nose. It was Pugglemud, hiding amongst the rocks like a spider. He looked worse than ever, for his clothes had been ripped to shreds. He was even missing a boot.

"I guess even the sea didn't want you," Kendra remarked as Pugglemud scrambled up the rocks and plopped his great weight next to her. "It coughed you up, did it? Lucky me."

Then another loud, piercing squawk came and Kendra looked back at the wreckage. One of the Krake soldiers was waddling right in their direction. Quickly, Kendra ducked down behind the boulder and shot Pugglemud a fierce glance. "Do you have any weapons?"

Pugglemud shook his head and wrung his hands. "What we goin' ta do? I can't be endin' up in no pit!"

Kendra plucked at her braids. "How about my wand?" she asked. "Do you still have it?"

Pugglemud reached into his coat and pulled out her stick of Eenwood. "Why would I give this to you?" he demanded.

"Oh, I don't know," Kendra retorted. "Maybe so we don't end up as dinner in the Rumble Pit?"

He tossed it to her and Kendra sighed in relief. It felt good to have the wand in her grasp. "I'll take my ring, too," she added.

Pugglemud opened his mouth to argue, but Kendra just pointed her wand at him. With a grimace, he passed over the Kazah Stone.

It was at this moment that the Krake appeared, leaping over the rocks and landing squarely in front of Kendra. "Oohcha!" it snapped, brandishing a spear. "More-cha prisoneez!"

Kendra turned to flee, but Pugglemud stuck out his spindly leg and tripped her. Like a lizard, he skittered over her and disappeared into the rocks. Quickly, Kendra rolled over and faced the Krake.

"Eenee no fightzee or get-cha chomps," the lizard-like creature hissed, its beak dripping with venom.

"Chomp on this," Kendra growled, lifting her wand and blasting the beast with a bolt of lightning. It struck him so hard that his helmet flew off and he fell back in a daze.

Kendra didn't wait for him to regain his wits. She turned and fled into the maze of boulders and almost immediately came upon Pugglemud, who was sitting on the ground nursing his foot. "I done sprained me ankle," he moaned. "Ya hafta help me."

"Like you helped me?" Kendra balked. "I'd start crawling if I were you. There'll be more Krakes on the way."

Pugglemud continued to whimper, but Kendra just kept climbing over the rocks, trying to put as much distance as possible between her and the vile dwarf. It was tough going, but she was thankful for the high boulders, for they hid her from view. Eventually she came to a spot where she could see through the rocks, and she paused to look down at the shore. The bulk of the Krake soldiers had left the beach, taking with them their newfound prisoners. Kendra knew where they were headed: to the dungeons, where they would await the next terrible fight in the Rumble Pit.

Kendra sighed. She had her wand and the Kazah Stone, but she needed one more important thing before she could jump to a different time: Oki. And to find him she would have to go into the castle.

CHAPTER 31

Kendra Hears the Call of Despair

Have you ever felt like you've experienced a situation before? There's a French expression to describe this sensation, déjà vu, which means, "already seen." Well, there was no doubt that Kendra was experiencing a strong sense of déjà vu as she reached the menacing walls of Krake Castle. She had been here before. She had already snuck through its gloomy corridors. And yet, here she was, about to do it all over again.

With a deep breath Kendra slipped through a grate and plodded up the drainage system towards the castle's core. Eventually she ended up in a large, warm chamber. She remembered this place; it was right above the royal hatchery, where hundreds of the Queen's enormous eggs were waiting to crack open with a new brood of Krakelings. Just thinking of it caused Kendra to give her braids a nervous yank. But here was the problem: last time she had found her way to the dungeons by going to the hatchery first.

I'm not doing that this time, Kendra vowed. *For once, I'm the one who doesn't want to think about eggs.*

Then Kendra realized there was one thing different from before. This time she had her wand. Holding it in her hands, she found a dark corner and closed her eyes in meditation, just like Uncle Griffinskitch had taught her. She let the sensations of the dungeon come to her. Soon she could hear it, see it, smell it, all in her mind. It wasn't difficult; there was a lot to be felt in that wretched place. She could hear desperate whimpers and wails, smell the fetid stench of the dungeon cells, even feel the onerous weight of chains.

A few minutes later, Kendra opened her eyes and let the wand guide her towards the despair. Part of her was screaming to turn and flee this place of anguish. But she was determined. She needed to find the dungeon. She needed to find Oki.

She snuck down passageways and across chasms, all the while feeling the temperature grow colder. In due course, she arrived at the colossal doorway that was the entrance to the dungeons. The door was meant for creatures larger than herself, so she easily slipped underneath it and into the dark tunnel beyond.

After one more nervous pull on her longest braid, she crept ahead. On one side of the passage she could see the prison cells that held the would-be gladiators as they awaited the next rumble. There were all sorts of strange creatures, just like last time—fierce ones, ones that could gobble her down with a single gulp. Many of them clutched at her as she slipped past; she kept to the far wall and followed the curve of the passage as it spiraled downwards.

The first prisoner she found from the circus was the peryton. He stared at her from his cell, but now his eyes no longer held the slightest glimmer of arrogance. One of his wings hung limply at his side; Kendra guessed it had been broken in the shipwreck.

The peryton looked at Kendra in earnest warning and whispered, "Careful. A guard comes."

Kendra hugged the shadows, knowing enough to trust the peryton's keen instincts. Sure enough, a Krake soldier soon came scuttling around the bend of the passage. In one claw was a ring of rusty keys and in the other, hanging upside down by his tail, was Oki. The Krake was just about to toss the mouse into a cell when he spotted Kendra.

The creature's eyes widened in surprise, but in an instant Kendra raised her wand and unleashed a bolt that caused the Krake to collapse, dropping both Oki and the dungeon keys. The bird-like beast gave his head a shake, then picked himself up to glare at Kendra, as if contemplating a fight. All it took was for Kendra to brandish her wand and the Krake instantly fled down the corridor.

Kendra helped Oki to his feet. "Are you okay?"

"It's like a nightmare," he moaned. "How did we ever end up back here?"

"It'll all be over soon," she assured him. "I'm going to get us out of here."

229

"Then you must hurry," came a voice. "The guard will sound the alarm and you'll soon be overrun by these dreadful monsters."

Kendra turned to see her mother standing in the cell next to the peryton. She looked worse than ever, for her face was streaked with grime and her eyes were heavy with dark circles. Quickly, Kendra snatched the keys that the guard had dropped and hurried to unlock her mother's cell.

"What are you doing?" Kayla demanded. "You must leave. There's not a moment to lose."

"I have Kazah," Kendra explained as she found the right key and turned it with a satisfying click. "I can jump anytime."

"What's the use?" Oki said in a despondent tone. "We can't jump physical distance. Even if we jump back to when your mom was a Teenling, we'll still be *here,* in the castle."

"That can't be helped," Kendra said. "We'll have to make our way back to the Forests of Wretch from here."

"How?" Oki squeaked. "It's across sea and forest and . . ."

"We'll just have to do it," Kendra insisted. "It's the only way."

"No," Kayla declared, stepping out into the prison corridor. "There may be another."

"What are you talking about?" Kendra asked.

"In the time you remember, you survived the Rumble Pit," Kayla said. "Your uncle was there, and your friends. Right?"

Kendra and Oki looked at each other, then nodded.

"So you must try and return to that time," Kayla said.

"What are you talking about?" Kendra asked. "Does that time even exist? Isn't it erased? How can that timeline be there until we go and fix it?"

"It's still there," her mother answered. "Look." She hunted around the straw spread sparsely around her cell, found three twigs, and arranged them so that they looked like a sideways Y. "See?" Kayla said. "It's like this. Once I read your letter, time branched into two separate lines. Now this time and the one you know—the one you remember—are both moving forward, running parallel. Both timelines exist. Two alternate realities."

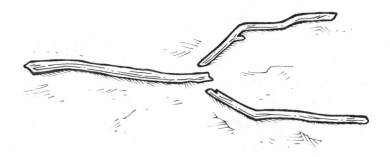

"It makes my head spin," Kendra groaned.

"I know," Kayla said. "But this alternate timeline still exists. Trust me. You must keep it real in your mind. And you must jump to it."

"This is *kolookookoo*," Oki exclaimed. "It's not jumping backwards *or* forward. It's like . . . jumping *across*."

"Exactly," Kayla said. "If you jump backwards in this time-line, we have no idea what kind of situation you'll be in. But if you can jump to the timeline you know, there'll be someone there to help you. This much is certain."

"Are you sure this jump is possible?" Kendra asked.

"The mysteries of Kazah are deep," her mother said. "Nearly thirty-five years have passed since you met me as a Teenling. Since then, I've devoted my life to the study of

Kazah magic. And I think this jump can be accomplished. But it will be complicated. You'll need to find a quiet, safe place to concentrate."

"But—,"

"There's no time to argue," Kayla interrupted and, as if to punctuate her warning, the squawks of approaching Krakes now filled the corridor. "See?" Kayla said. "They're coming."

"Eek! We'll never escape now!" Oki squealed.

"Yes, you will," Kayla announced with sudden vigor in her voice. The keys were still hanging from her cell door, but she snatched them with a jangle. "I'm going to release the prisoners. All of them. The Krakes will have a real rumble to deal with—right here in the dungeons. That will give you two a chance to flee and enact the magic of Kazah."

"But—," Kendra started to say, when her mother grabbed her and hugged her tight.

"Listen," Kayla said, looking her straight in the eye. "I love you, Kendra. But you have to go."

"Wh-what about you?" Kendra asked.

"Don't worry about me," her mother replied. "I have a whole gaggle of slurp-sucking bird-brains to keep me amused."

"That's not what I meant!" Kendra persisted, even as the sounds of the approaching Krakes grew louder. "What's going to happen to you in this timeline? Shouldn't you just come with us?"

"No—I don't belong in your time any more than you belong here," Kayla said. Then she reached inside her robe and pulled out the tiny ragdoll rabbit.

Kendra had to blink. She couldn't imagine how Kayla had managed to hang onto the toy through all of their misfortunes.

"I want you to have this," her mother said.

"I'm a little old for dolls," Kendra said. "And, besides, that's not mine . . . it's the other Kendra's."

"I made this for someone I love with all my heart," Kayla declared. "And that someone is you."

Kendra stared into her mother's eyes. They were afire now, as if she was suddenly that Teenling girl again, the one who had single-handedly chased Captain Rinkle and his men through the dungeons of the Elder Stone.

Kayla tucked the ragdoll rabbit inside Kendra's robe, and then, without another word on the matter, turned and thrust the keys into the door of the peryton's cage. "GO!" she yelled over her shoulder, and there was such command in her voice that at once Kendra clutched Oki by the paw and scampered down the passageway.

Even as they rounded the corner, Kendra could hear the clangs of opening cages and the cheers of escaping prisoners. Only a moment later those cheers turned to shouts and screams, which could only mean one thing: the Krake guards had arrived on the scene. Kendra paused to listen as the passageway behind them reverberated with the sounds of battle.

"Come on," Kendra told Oki, wiping a stray tear from her eye. "We'd better hurry."

They climbed upwards, into the castle, with escaping prisoners—and the Krake guards—chasing after them. Kendra knew they had to get as far away as possible; she'd never be able to use the magic of the Kazah Stone unless she could concentrate. Frantically, she led Oki through the network of corridors, across bridges, and up spiraling staircases. Still, the chaos followed them.

It's difficult to pay attention to what's ahead of you when there's certain danger snapping at your heels. That's why Kendra didn't see the ventilation shaft in front of them. She and Oki tumbled into it headlong. Mercifully, it wasn't a straight drop; they slid at an angle, hitting a corner here and a bump there until at last they struck the ground. They found themselves in complete darkness.

"Where are we?" Oki wondered.

"I'm not sure," Kendra answered.

With a flourish of her hand, she caused her wand to glow, but it did little to vanquish the surrounding darkness. Kendra cocked her head and listened; she could still hear the din of the battle raging far above, but the sounds were muted and distant.

"I guess we're safe enough," Kendra said, slipping Kazah onto her finger. "This place is as good as any. Come on, put your paws over the Stone."

"Why? What's that going to do?" Oki asked.

"This is a difficult jump," Kendra explained. "I need your energy too. We both need to remember what it was like when we were in Krake Castle last time."

"How could I forget?" Oki grumbled, placing his paws on the Kazah Stone.

Kendra shut her eyes and began to breathe deeply. Her mind eventually became quiet, and she let her imagination take her to the time when she had first found herself in Krake Castle. She not only had to imagine the things she saw, heard, smelled, touched, or tasted—she had to connect with her feelings in a way she never had before. That was the tricky part, and she knew that's why she needed Oki's help. He was good at feeling.

At last, the Stone began to glow; Kendra could sense it even through her closed eyes. Then it began to tremble on her finger. It had never behaved that way before, but even though Kendra desperately wondered what was happening she didn't dare open her eyes to risk disrupting the magic. Now her whole body was quaking; she thought the ring might fly right from her finger. She felt herself spinning, as if something was swinging her round and round, with such force that tears began to run from her eyes. Suddenly there was a thunderous crack—it felt as if for a moment Kendra had left her stomach behind—and the next thing she knew, she was sitting in something warm and soft.

Mud. She opened her eyes and found herself in a mound of thick purple sludge. Heaps of the stuff were piled around them.

"What happened?" Oki asked woozily.

Kendra lifted her hand and looked down at the Kazah Stone. The crack was so wide that it looked as if it might just crumble apart. "That jump nearly ripped Kazah in two," she gasped, wiping perspiration from her forehead (which was suddenly very hot).

Then, through the darkness, there was another sound. *Creeeeak!*

"What was that?" Oki asked anxiously. "The ring again?"

Kendra shook her head and listened.

Creeeeack! Craaaack! Creeeeak!

"It sounds more like . . . *oh no*," Kendra groaned. She began climbing the nearest mound of mud.

"What?" Oki asked, following after her.

Together, they reached the top of the slope, only to have the mud give way beneath their feet so that they slid down the other side. They landed with a plop amidst a cluster of giant, round . . . things.

Kendra gasped. They had arrived right smack in the middle of the Krake hatchery and at the worst possible moment. Around them, as far as the eye could see, was an endless stretch of enormous eggs—and they were all about to hatch.

CHAPTER 32

Danger Hatches in the Castle of Krakes

Monsters are born dangerous. They're hungry and vicious and they will rip you limb from limb if you so happen to be in their way. And when it comes to monsters, some say there are none more dangerous than a brood of freshly hatched Krakelings. They might not yet have their venom, but their beaks are still as sharp and jagged as saw blades. Add to this the fact that they hatch in the hundreds, and you can begin to picture the predicament of our heroes.

"It's . . . it's . . . *eggoriffic*," Oki gulped.

"Oki," Kendra whispered. "Please don't tell me you were thinking of eggs when we jumped."

Oki's only reply was to nervously twitch his tail.

237

"Let me guess," Kendra said. "You thought about Krake eggs, and then you thought about them hatching."

"Well, actually, I was trying *not* to think about them hatching," Oki said sheepishly.

"You can't NOT think of something!" Kendra cried.

"I couldn't help it!" Oki squealed. "Besides, we must have been in the hatchery all along—we were going to end up here no matter what I was thinking about."

"It's not the *where* I'm upset about so much as the *when*," Kendra said. "Krake eggs probably only hatch every couple of years, and here we are at the worst possible moment." Her frustration was punctuated by a loud shriek from the egg nearest to her.

"And just exactly *when* are we?" Oki fretted. "Did it work? Are we back in our own timeline?"

"I don't know; I think we've got bigger worries right now," Kendra replied, for now a large piece of the eggshell in front of her splintered away to reveal the beady yellow eye of a baby Krake.

Then, to make matters worse, an entire section of the wall behind the egg seemed to shift and move and—to her horror—Kendra realized it was no wall at all, but rather the gargantuan shape of Queen Krake.

The great bird-like beast towered over her eggs like a mountain next to a field of pebbles. She was so large, in fact, that all Kendra could really see of her was her massive head. This was covered in feathery purple fur, except at the top, where three long tendrils snaked upwards like crooked weather vanes. Then there was her beak, lined with serrated teeth and dripping with strings of drool. Worst of all were her eyes. She had one on each side of her head like a chicken, and they gleamed like mirrors.

Kendra could sense an "eek" building in Oki. Quickly, she cupped her hand over his mouth and pulled him back, searching desperately for the shadows.

But the queen didn't spot them. Indeed, she seemed to have eyes only for her hatching babies. She lowered her giant head and chirped, "Erk erk erk! Mama Krake love little koo-chi-koos! Mama must go watchee Rumba Pit, but little hatcheez comezee watch after munchee-munchee!"

Then, with a cackle, she lumbered away into the darkness.

"Munchee-munchee?" Oki worried, pulling Kendra's hand away from his mouth.

"I think she means *dinner*," Kendra whispered.

"That means owie-owie for us," Oki said.

"Krakes don't eat Eens," Kendra replied.

"Oh, good—I'll make sure to tell these *hugongous* babies before they gobble us up," Oki groaned.

"Come on. We better shake a braid."

She turned in the mud, slipped, and fell. It was then that she realized she was still wearing the Kazah Stone. It was so fractured and delicate that she knew she needed to take extra care with it. Gently, she slipped it inside her robe.

You just need to last a little longer, she thought.

"Eek!" Oki suddenly squealed.

Kendra looked up. In an explosion of shell and slimy green yolk, a baby Krake burst from the nearest egg, followed by the next, and so on and so on, as if each one was triggering the next like a row of firecrackers. In only a matter of seconds they were surrounded by hundreds of squealing Krakelings. Then, suddenly, they went quiet. Every neck went erect as the creatures lifted their beaks to the air and sniffed.

"They can smell food," Kendra guessed.

"Us?" Oki gasped.

It was something else; Kendra could smell it too, a disgusting, rotten stench wafting in from behind them. Then, as if on a signal, the Krakelings tore across the chamber in a stampede of claws and snapping beaks.

"We're in their way!" Kendra screamed.

She desperately waved her wand to raise some sort of shield, but she wasn't quick enough. They were caught up in the swell of baby Krakes, pushed ahead as if at the front of some dreadful tidal wave. They were bounced and jostled (it was all Kendra could do to hang onto her wand) until at last they found themselves pushed right into some sort of giant trough filled with what one could only describe as slop.

Whatever it was, the Krakelings found it delicious. Their sharp beaks zipped in and out of the trough, pecking for every last morsel. It seemed by miracle alone that Kendra and Oki weren't torn to shreds. Kendra tucked her wand in her belt, grabbed Oki by the paw, and scrambled frantically towards the corner of the trough, trying to find safety. Down came the beak of another Krakeling—this time Kendra's cloak caught on one of his jagged teeth, and the next thing she knew, she and Oki were jerked upwards and sent sailing through the air.

They landed right on the backs of a pair of Krakelings.

"EEK!" Oki screamed.

"Hang on," Kendra told him. "This might be the safest place for us yet."

She squeezed her knees into her Krakeling and now it seemed the feeding frenzy was over. The babies were on the move again, this time charging through an open doorway and down a dark passageway. The Krakelings they were riding squawked murderously, twisting their heads as they desperately tried to reach them with their claws and beaks. Kendra and Oki hung on for dear life and the Krakelings, not wanting to be left behind by their brood, had no choice but to keep moving.

Onwards and upwards they went through the network of castle passages. This took considerable time, but eventually they

reached a large open gallery. Ahead of them, Kendra could see the metalwork of a giant, dome-shaped cage—and she knew at once where they had arrived.

The Rumble Pit.

Their Krakelings had fallen to the rear of the brood, so just as they reached the top of the arena seating gallery, Kendra and Oki jumped off and let the disgruntled babies rush after their fellow hatchlings.

"Thanks, little snappers," Kendra muttered.

They could hear the roars and shrieks from the Rumble Pit and Kendra's mind instantly flooded with a thousand terrifying memories. Desperately, she jerked on a braid.

"Kendra, we have to get out of here," Oki implored, trembling head to foot.

"F-first, I have to see it," Kendra said bravely. "If Kazah worked the way we wanted it to, then this should be the rumble we were at last time."

She crept a few steps forward and found herself at the very top of the arena's seating gallery. In front of her were rows of spectators—all Krakes—and past them, in the pit, was the terrible battle. But it wasn't the action in the pit that caught Kendra's attention—it was what was occurring on the royal balcony, where Queen Krake's throne stood. For here was a far more tumultuous battle, and one that Kendra knew all too well. Because it was *her* battle.

There, standing right in front of her eyes, was herself. Trooogul—her brother in Unger form—was there too. She watched in stunned fascination as the events unfolded before her. She watched as Trooogul charged amidst a hail of arrows and knocked the queen's throne over in a crash of stone. She watched herself find the Shard from Greeve lying on the ground and pick it up. She watched as Agent Lurk appeared and a fierce argument raged between Trooogul and Lurk, each of them clamoring to seize that dark piece of stone. Then Queen Krake rose from the wreckage of her throne and began pounding her tail against the pavilion, smashing it to bits.

A sudden realization struck Kendra. She remembered this moment in the Rumble Pit—and so do you, if you were there the first time with Kendra. Something strange had happened, something that had spooked the Krake warriors and caused the queen to disappear. Kendra had never known what it was—until now.

"I'm here for a reason," she declared, for she could feel her spark again, urging her. She spun around and looked at Oki. "Stay put," she said decisively.

"What are you going to do?" he squealed. "Don't interfere in the timeline again."

"This time I have to," she said. "Trust me."

She bounded down the stairs and through the seating gallery, Krakes marking her progress with squawks of surprise.

Then she jumped and landed on the crumbling pavilion, just as the other Kendra was sent sprawling backwards into the seats, surrounded by a swarm of Krakes. Kendra pulled out her wand and now everyone—Queen Krake, the drones, even Trooogul—was staring at her in surprise. Kendra knew they were all wondering the same thing: how could she be in two places at once?

And then, because Kendra knew she could do it—because, from her perspective, she *had already* done it—she performed magic beyond her humble means. Falling to her knees, she cast the words inside her mind and brought her tiny wand against the stone pavilion. There was a loud crack and a blinding flare of light—then the opposite end of the platform split into massive angular slabs. These toppled downwards, smashing through the dome over the Rumble Pit and into the fracas below. With them went the queen. For a desperate moment she clawed and scraped at the side of the pit, but all was in vain. She plunged into the middle of that terrible battle, now no longer a spectator, but one of the many fighting for survival.

The rest of the Krake drones—those surrounding the other Kendra or watching this whole scene unfold—now scattered in a terrified cacophony of shrieks and squawks.

The remaining part of the pavilion was tilting, threatening to follow the other half into the pit. Agent Lurk was nowhere to be found, but Kendra could see Trooogul balancing himself on a chunk of unstable stone. The great Unger was still staring at her with enormous eyes, bewildered beyond all belief.

Kendra didn't wait for him to react. She knew he would save himself. She leapt back into the seating gallery, near to where her other self was still lying on her back. She didn't

give that Kendra a chance to see her; quickly she bounded up the stairs, back towards Oki. She knew her other self would be confused. She would pull herself to her feet to find the pavilion destroyed, Queen Krake gone, and her drones scattered.

Just as I remember it, Kendra thought.

Two days later, Kendra and Oki were sitting on a mountain ridge, staring out across the Seas of Ire. They had found their way out of the castle (not without some difficulty) and had wandered across the craggy cliffs until their legs could carry them no farther.

Even though she had not stayed to witness it, Kendra knew everything had unfolded in the arena as she remembered. Ratchet's cloud ship had come with Uncle Griffinskitch to save the peryton—and herself—from death. Now, somewhere out there, the *Big Bang* was flying across the skies, headed for the City on the Storm in search of Trooogul. And eventually it would be attacked by Agent Lurk and his skarm.

That Kendra's adventure is about to start, Kendra thought. *Mine is coming to a finish.*

"What now?" Oki asked.

"I think we have to go back in time and steal that letter from my mother," Kendra said.

"Why?" Oki asked. "If we're in this timeline, doesn't that mean everything's all right?"

"Maybe," Kendra pondered. "Or maybe it's just like what happened in the Rumble Pit. I saved myself. If I hadn't, then everything might have turned out differently."

"So we have to snatch the letter," Oki said. "It'll solidify the timeline."

Just how my hundred-and-twelve-year-old self would put it, Kendra thought. Then she sat cross-legged on the rocks, closed her eyes, raised her wand, and breathed deeply. Her mind settled, she sent a magic whisper across the wind:

Hear my call, one to reign,
In time of need, time of pain.
Then wing across wind and rain;
Oh, come to me, Aurius Feyn.

"What was that about?" Oki asked after she had opened her eyes.

"Don't worry," Kendra answered. "Everything is all right."

"Not exactly," Oki fretted. "If we're going to get that letter from your mother, we have to find our way to the Forests of Wretch. And between us and where we need to go there's an entire sea. How are we going to cross it?"

Kendra saw a small dot appear on the skyline. "Why, that's simple," she told Oki with a smile. "We're going to fly."

CHAPTER 33

The Last Gasp of Kazah

It was the peryton. Kendra watched in awe as he soared towards them, across the clouds. He was a bold and beautiful creature, and she wondered if she would ever cease to be amazed by his majesty. He circled above them, once, twice, then at last landed next to them, gracefully as a feather.

"Arinotta!" he exclaimed, calling Kendra by his pet name for her. "Were those your words I heard on the breath of the wind?"

Kendra nodded.

"Fur and feathers!" he uttered. "I am confused. Only an hour ago I bid farewell to you on that flying ship."

"It's a bit hard to explain," Kendra said. "But from my perspective . . . well, that was much longer ago than an hour."

"You can say that again," Oki added.

"By the king's wings!" the peryton snorted. "Some underling magic, I suspect."

Kendra smiled. "I need your help, Prince."

"My wings are yours, Arinotta. What foe might I vanquish for you?"

"Just distance," Kendra replied. "We need to go to a place far away from here. Can you take us?"

"Certainly," said the peryton. "Climb aboard my back, and we shall make all speed."

They used a nearby outcropping of rock to climb aboard the back of the regal stag. When they were secure, the magnificent peryton rustled his wings, and with a snort he galloped into the air.

This journey did not happen all at once, of course, nor did it happen without incident. It was winter, after all, and they fought not only weather, but hunger, and exhaustion too. For five days they travelled over sea and mountain, forest and valley, finding shelter and food on the ground below whenever necessary. At last, one bleak afternoon, Oki recognized some peaks in the distance.

"Those are the Crags of Dredge," he called to the peryton. "Be careful; it's where the skarm nest."

"Perytons are kings of the sky," the great deer declared. "My heart shudders not at the thought of skarm."

"If those are the Crags of Dredge, then below are the Forests of Wretch," Kendra said. "We're where we need to be."

The peryton circled to the ground and landed in the drifts of snow.

"I smell danger," the stag remarked. "Some creatures hunt nearby."

"Eek!" Oki squealed. "Probably Goojuns."

"Worry not," Prince declared. "They are no match for my antlers."

"We won't be here long," Kendra said.

She tried to send the peryton on his way, but he would not leave until he was sure they were safe. So Kendra said her good-byes, warned him of the magic she was about to perform, and settled down in the icy shadows of the forest to call upon the power of Kazah.

With Oki holding tight to her cloak, Kendra thought of her mother, the tempestuous Teenling whom she had left in the very spot she was now sitting. She thought of the letter that she had written to her. More importantly, she felt the emotion that she had poured into that letter. It took only moments for the Kazah Stone to tremble to life; indeed, its crack was now so wide that it quickly sucked Kendra and Oki through its fissure.

In an instant they found themselves in the warm summer sun. The peryton, of course, was no longer anywhere to be seen, for they had traveled into the past.

"Gayla?" Kendra called out.

"Braids?" Gayla appeared from behind a tree trunk. "What are you still doing here? Aren't you going back to your own time?"

"In a moment," Kendra said, charging up to Gayla to embrace her. As she did so, she snuck one hand into the pocket of the Teenling's robe and, with a sigh of relief, felt the scrap of parchment. Stealthily, she plucked it out and slipped it down her sleeve.

"Hmph," Gayla grunted, as she wriggled free of Kendra's grasp. "*Another* hug? That's what I get for letting you hug me the first time. You come back for more. Yeesh."

"Gayla!" came the sound of Uncle Griffinskitch's voice from beyond the bushes.

"Look, I ought to go," Gayla declared. "Maybe I'll see you twiddle-twins around sometime."

Kendra nodded. "Gayla?"

"What?"

"Just . . . just be you," Kendra said.

"Sure," the girl said, casting her a strange look.

Then she was gone. Kendra quickly turned to Oki and triumphantly showed him the letter.

"Thank the ancients," Oki sighed. "I guess we can leave now."

"Just a minute," Kendra said, putting a finger to her lips. She wanted to hear what would happen between Uncle Griffinskitch and her mother. She ducked down low in the bushes, pulling Oki with her.

"Gayla," came the sound of Uncle Griffinskitch's voice. "Where in the name of Een have you been?"

"Relax," Gayla said. "Hey—what's *he* doing here?"

Kendra and Oki looked at each other in surprise. *Burdock?* Kendra mouthed to Oki, but the little mouse only shrugged. Though they couldn't see through the foliage, Gayla's next words solved the mystery.

"Krimson, don't you know there's Goojuns prowling around out here?" the spirited Teenling girl demanded. "They could pluck you like a rose."

"Humph," Uncle Griffinskitch muttered. "Leave the boy alone."

"Since when are you on *his* side?" Gayla asked.

"Since he told me that you like to sneak out here," Uncle Griffinskitch replied. "Which, by the way, is going to come to a stop. But we can discuss that later. For now, let us return home. The boy promised to cook us dinner if we actually found you."

"Er . . . what about Burdock?" Gayla asked.

"Humph," came Uncle Griffinskitch's reply, and Kendra knew that type of humph all too well. It meant, "Don't worry about that. Don't worry at all."

"Well, garden boy," Gayla said cheerfully. "I sure hope you know how to cook. Because let me tell you, I've got a *monster* of an appetite. And when I say monster, I mean monster . . . "

Her voice faded away. Kendra smiled at Oki. "Everything should be put right now. Let's get back to when we belong."

"*Foogiewunda!*" Oki cheered.

The Kazah Stone was still on Kendra's finger, and she closed her eyes and concentrated once more. Oki clutched her sleeve.

The Stone rumbled and grumbled. Even as she thought of her time—the cloud ship, Uncle Griffinskitch, Ratchet, the professor, and Jinx—she could feel Kazah rip, rend, and roar upon her finger. Suddenly there was a resounding snap—and when Kendra next opened her eyes the Stone was completely split in two, burst open like a kernel of popcorn on her finger. She knew the last of the Stone's magic had been exhausted.

"Oh!" Oki exclaimed when he saw the Stone. "I hope we're in the right time."

"Me, too," Kendra said, tugging on a braid. "Because no matter what, we're here to stay. Well, come on. Let's see if we can find the cloud ship."

The snow was deep, but if you're as light as an Een and the

snow has had time to form a crust, you can walk right across it, which is exactly what Kendra and Oki did, all the while staring up through the branches to see if they could catch a glimpse of the *Big Bang*. Kendra remembered that they had originally time-jumped from the ship during the night and she suspected that their friends hadn't even noticed them missing until the morning. She wondered how long ago that was from the crew's perspective. One day? Two? She had no way of knowing.

She pulled out her wand and sent a plea across the wind. *Uncle Griffinskitch? Are you there? We've fallen to the ground. We're down in the Forests of Wretch!*

Then she heard a reply: *We're coming.* At least, she thought that's what she heard. *Perhaps it was my imagination,* Kendra thought anxiously. It was so bitterly cold she could hardly concentrate. She tucked the wand back into her belt and buried her hands inside her robe.

They trudged onwards. The sky was growing dark and gloomy, and soon the snow swirled about them, obscuring their vision.

"We wouldn't see the cloud ship if it was right above our heads," Oki complained. "What are we going to do?"

Kendra didn't know. Then some dark shape caught her eye through the whirling flakes and she squinted hard. In the next moment, Jinx materialized from the haze of falling snow and came skidding to a halt right in front of them.

I hope it's not the happy, kind Jinx, Kendra thought. *Otherwise we're not in the right timeline.*

"Well, well, well," Jinx said with a scowl. "If it isn't Madame Braid-Brain and her trusty sidekick, Sir Eeksalot. How in the name of all things Een did you two halfwit, maggot-minded muddle-heads manage to fall out of your cribs all the way to the ground? What a couple of snow-sucking snotheads! I've been freezing my ankles off all morning looking for you."

"Oh, thank the ancients!" Kendra exclaimed.

And she rushed forward and threw her arms around the grumpy grasshopper.

CHAPTER 34

An Enchanted Gift

There's nothing sweeter than a reunion with old friends. Once Kendra was aboard the cloud ship, she made a great fuss over the crew. She was glad to see that they were exactly as they should be. Jinx's words were sharp, the professor's were long, and Ratchet's were full of nonsense. As for Uncle Griffinskitch's words—well, they were mostly humphs. This made Kendra perfectly happy, of course, because it meant he was alive. She couldn't bear to think of the alternate timeline where he had perished. Indeed, she hugged the old wizard so tightly that she nearly squeezed him right out of his beard.

"I don't know what's gotten into you," he grunted.

"Oh, Uncle Griffinskitch," she said, gazing at him in earnest. "I have so much to tell you."

"Humph," he muttered softly, a knowing look in his eye. "All in good time. For now, you need rest. *And a bath.*"

Kendra smiled. She knew she looked a sight, with her robe in tatters and her hair a tangle. She passed the broken Kazah Stone over to her uncle and said, "Here, keep this for me." Then she went with Oki below deck where they devoured bowls of delicious carrot soup, took hot baths, and collapsed into their beds.

How long Kendra slept, she didn't know, but when she awoke it was to find Oki's bed empty. She assumed her industrious friend was already up and relating his adventures to Ratchet. Kendra's clothes had been washed and mended, and were now waiting for her at the end of her bunk.

The work of Professor Bumble-bean, I suppose, she thought.

It felt wonderful to put on something clean. After she had dressed, Kendra slipped out into the corridor of the ship and almost immediately bumped into Jinx. The grasshopper was carrying a steaming bowl of soup.

"There's more in the galley if you want it," the grasshopper announced. "This one's for *Agent Quirk.*" She gestured at the door to the nearby storage room.

"Oh," Kendra said with a start. She had almost forgotten that Leerlin Lurk was still their prisoner. "Here," Kendra said, reaching for the bowl. "I'll take it to him."

"Suit yourself," Jinx said with a shrug. "Your uncle put a spell on the door so that he can't sneak out—plus another one to make sure his cloak won't work inside the room. But be careful—that boy is still dangerous."

Kendra nodded. After an anxious moment of staring at the storage room door, she turned the handle and stepped inside. There was Leerlin Lurk, hunched in the corner, gnashing his teeth. He looked more loathsome than ever for, of course, Kendra now had the picture of the golden-haired Leerlin in her mind, that handsome Teenling who had paraded so arrogantly before Oki's council.

"What do you want, girl?" Agent Lurk hissed, his one good eye burning with fury.

"I brought you something to eat," she said, setting the bowl down on the floor and stepping away. She couldn't help but to treat him as if he were a wild animal; in so many ways he looked like one.

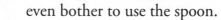

Lurk skittered forward, sniffed at the contents of the bowl, then began to slurp it down. He didn't even bother to use the spoon.

"Are you going to sit here all day and stare at me?" he growled between gulps. "I guess you like a good freak show."

"I'm not staring," Kendra said. "And I've been in a freak show myself. There might be a way to help you, you know. Uncle Griffinskitch helped the peryton once, in the Rumble Pit. He fixed his antlers and healed his wings."

"So what?" Lurk scowled. "I wouldn't let that old fool of a wizard anywhere near me with his wand. Magic can't fix everything."

"I know," Kendra said, remembering the words her old, blind self had once told her. "But we could try to help. You don't need to be in pain."

"Pah! My only pain, girl, is to sit here and listen to your worthless babble," he retorted. "You think you are so wise. What do you know about the world?"

Kendra sighed. "More than you give me credit for," she said. "And in many ways, it's thanks to you."

Lurk's only reply was to hiss. He finished his soup and dropped the bowl to the floor with a clatter. Kendra collected it and left the troubled boy to glower. After returning the bowl to the galley, she made her way up to the deck of the ship.

It was a cold day, and the skies were clear and crisp. She stood at the railing and stared across the clouds. After a moment she heard footsteps and turned to see Professor Bumblebean approaching her.

"I do say, Kendra," the cheerful scholar greeted. "You do look better for your rest."

"Thank you," Kendra replied.

"By the way," Professor Bumblebean said, "I discovered this in one of your pockets when I was laundering your robe. How did you happen upon it?"

He was holding the ragdoll rabbit.

"Oh!" Kendra remarked, taking the scruffy toy. "I . . . well, it was a gift."

"It's an Een toy," the professor said. "Very special."

"I never had one as a child," Kendra said. "What makes it so special?"

"My word! Een toys are invested with certain magic," the Professor explained happily. "They are stuffed with the cotton of the famous cloudtail plant. That cotton, you see, absorbs all the love of the mother who constructs the toy. That toy then binds itself to the first child who loves it. I do say, an Een toy offers bountiful comfort to an Eenling, especially if the mother is absent. So you see, Kendra, you have received a very special gift—though, I might say, you seem somewhat old for dolls."

Kendra laughed. "Yes . . . I know."

"Well, I best coordinate my latest calculations with Ratchet," the professor declared. "I think I might have discovered the exact location of this mysterious City on the Storm. With any fortune, we shall maunder no further, and our journey will come to an expeditious conclusion." With this said, he gave a cheerful whistle and ambled across the deck, leaving Kendra to her thoughts.

Kendra stared down at the ragdoll and touched one of its long, floppy ears. Was it really magical? She held it close to her chest—and at once felt the most amazing sensation flood through her body. It was almost impossible to describe. The only way Kendra could think of it was as if someone had suddenly lifted her from her feet and dunked her into a giant pool of comfort and joy. She wasn't sure she had ever felt such warmth before. Then she knew at once: those feelings came from her mother.

"Thank you," she whispered.

"Kendra? Are you okay?" It was Oki, who had come to join her at the railing.

"I'm better than I've been for a long time," Kendra told the mouse. She tucked the rabbit away, and together she and Oki stared out at the glorious blue sky. Somewhere out there, Kendra knew, was the City on the Storm—and her brother.

"Well, here we are," Oki said presently, "standing on the *Big Bang* and gazing out at the clouds. Just like before. It's like nothing happened."

Kendra looked at him and smiled. "Except for everything," she said.

The End

TIMELINE, showing important dates in the HISTORY of EEN

Note: Dates are arranged according to the Een calendar and have no correspondence with history as recorded by the outside world.

The FIRST AGE of EEN (The DAYS of EEN)

year 1 — The Lands of Een founded by the elves from the west.

y.446 — Leemus Longshanks is born.

y.515 — First Council of Elders formed, consisting of the seven brothers of Een.

y.522 — Grendel Greeve banished by the Brothers of Een.

y.524 — Grendel Greeve builds the Door to Unger and his temple maze.

y.525 — Leemus Longshanks and the brothers travel to the temple of Grendel Greeve with their armies.

Grendel Greeve casts his curse upon his brothers and their armies; only Leemus Longshanks escapes.

Founding of the five monster tribes: Ungers, Krakes, Goojuns, Orrids, and Izzards.

Leemus Longshanks returns to the Lands of Een to build the Magic Curtain, hiding Een from the outside world.

Creation of the Een Guard and appointment of the first Captain of the Guard, Clovin Cloudfoot.

End of the First Age of Een.

The SECOND AGE of EEN

year 1 — The first Jamboreen is held on the banks of the River Wink.

y.27 — Leemus Longbraids passes away.

y.76 — Construction of the Elder Stone is completed.

y.125 — Flavius Faun arrives in Een.

y.130 — The first celebration of Ald Meryn's Eve.

y.140 — Flavius Faun passes away; the town of Faun's End is named in his honor.

y.998 — The elders construct the Box of Whispers.

263

	y.999	Discovering that a dragon egg is about to hatch in the treasure chambers of the Elder Stone, the sorceress Esme Evermoon is sent to cast the egg into the wilds of the outside world.
	y.1275	Byron Bumblebean founds the Library of Een in the town of Faun's End.
	y.1920	Gregor Griffinskitch is born.
	y.1950	Gayla Griffinskitch is born; her parents, Galia and Grumbel Griffinskitch pass away.
	y.1977	Gayla Griffinskitch marries Krimson Kandlestar, changing her name to Kayla Kandlestar.
	y.1980	Kiro Kandlestar is born.
	y.1987	Kendra Kandlestar is born.
	y.1988	The Kandlestar family disappears in the outside world; Gregor Griffinskitch adopts Kendra.
	y.1998	The Box of Whispers is stolen (late summer); Gregor Griffinskitch leads a company into the outside world to recover it.
	y.1999	Kendra travels to the Greeven Wastes to seek the Door to Unger (late spring).
		The temple maze and the Door to Unger are destroyed (early summer).
		A war amongst the five monster tribes erupts.
		Kendra apprentices to Gregor Griffinskitch to study Een magic and receives her own wand of Eenwood (late summer).
		Kendra takes the Shard from Greeve and travels to Krake Castle to seek her brother.
		Kendra fights in the Rumble Pit.
	y.2000	Kendra and the crew of the *Big Bang* seek the City on the Storm.
		End of the Second Age of Een.

The THIRD AGE of EEN

	year 1	The new Council of Elders is formed.
	y.46	Shaden Shiverbone is born.
	y.86	Leerlin Lurk is born.
	y.99	Leerlin Lurk steals the Kazah Stone and the shadow cloak from his master, the Wizard Shiverbone.

264

THE
CHRONICLES
OF
KENDRA
KANDLESTAR

Book 1: The Box of Whispers
Book 2: The Door to Unger
Book 3: The Shard from Greeve
Book 4: The Crack in Kazah
Book 5: The Search for Arazeen

Visit
www.kendrakandlestar.com
for activities, teacher guides, news, and to
send an Een-mail to Lee Edward Födi

Readers Respond
to Kendra Kandlestar

* ⭐ *

Lee Edward Födi shares some of his favorite letters

I love your books! My favorite character is Jinx. She is really funny. I also like Kendra and Oki. I really don't have a favorite of your books. They are all fantastic. I have one question. How did you come up with the Rumble Pit, and all of the other places Kendra and her friends go? Please, keep writing I can't wait until your new book comes out.

~ Iris, age 9

I just finished your books. I hope you make another book. I like Kendra, Oki, Captain Jinx, Uncle Griffinskitch, Professor Bumblebean, and Ratchet.

~ Ryan, age 10

Hi, it's your Eeny fan (ha ha). Well, I think Eens are real. I'm going to be an Een for HallowEEN, maybe Kiro or Uncle Griffinskitch. I'm glad you're making a fourth book.

~ Luke, age 9

You are my favorite author. Your books are too awesome! I think I got Kendra Kandlestar fever. My favorite book is the third book. You are also the greatest illustrator I know.

~ Herald, age 10

My favorite book is *The Crack in Kazah* because Kendra and Oki travel back in time. My favorite characters are Pugglemud and Oki because Pugglemud always does bad things to Kendra and her family, but everything turns out alright in the end because Pugglemud always gets defeated afterwards. I like Oki because he is really cute and the complete opposite of Pugglemud, and because he always tries not to think about things (like eggs), but it never works.

~ Calulla, age 11

I was wondering when the next book is coming out? I LOVE YOUR BOOKS the last one was amazing. I loved it! I can't wait to read the next book. It only took me three days to read it and I loved it. Your biggest fan.

~ Lauren, age 12

My friend got me to read your books and I LOVE them! I am only on the first book but it is my favorite book for now in the series. My favorite character is Kendra of course. You are an awesome writer! From your number one fan!

~ Emily, age 11

Kendra Kandlestar is a great book for anyone. I love how it's filled with magical creatures and magical things.

~ Kendra, age 11

Dear Mr. Wiz, I absolutely LOOOOOOOOOOOOVE your books. I read all three books in just two days! Please write the series until it reaches one thousand. Or I'll send you a whole carton of eggs and ketchup.

~ Angela, age 12

My favorite character is Kendra. I think she is really cool. Her braids are kind of like Pippi Longstocking's. I can't wait until the fifth book!

~ Nandita, age 10

Dear Mr. Fodi, your books are so splendidly amazing! My favorite book is *The Shard from Greeve*. I absolutely enjoyed the part when they entered the Rumble Pit. My favorite character is Prince because he is such a majestic creature!

~ Jordon, age 10

Hi Mr. Fodi, I am really eager to find out if they find Kiro or not. I love all your *Kendra Kandlestar* books. I have re-drawn some of your pictures and made them look a lot like the ones in the books. Thanks, from one of your biggest fans.

~ Haylee, age 10

I love your books and my favorite characters are Honest Oki, Kendra, and Prince Peryton.

~ Kathy, age 10

I really, really, really, loved your *Kendra Kandlestar* series! My favorite character is Kendra's uncle because he always said 'Humph.' Keep writing!

~ Andrew, age 12

I love your book *The Shard from Greeve*. It's amazing! I hope you write like one thousand more books! *The Box of Whispers* is very interesting! *The Door to Unger*, well, I was addicted to it! I also love all your illustrations from all three books.

~ Ella, age 9

I have now read all your books. I still can't believe that the thing Oki is most scared of is a pickle! Or was it because he was thinking about (or NOT thinking about) pickles? Plus, I don't think that Ratchet's inventions are rubbish. (In fact I would help him work out the kinks!)

~ Yash, age 9

Can you put this message in your next book? I just love the *Kendra Kandlestar* series! I'm the book's biggest fan! I even have a costume!

~ Jenny, age 9

I love your series, *Kendra Kandlestar*! I was wondering when the next book is coming out, because I really want to read it.

~ Saige, age 13

I love your *Kendra Kandlestar* series. I really love your books. How do you think of these brilliant ideas? My mom does twelve different voices for all the characters—it's awesome!

~ Madelyn, age 9

I love your *Kendra Kandlestar* books! They're always full of lots of adventure and suspense. My favorite character is Honest Oki. I'll think of turnips! Or onions! I also really like Uncle Griffinskitch. Humph!

~ Chloe, age 10

We really like your series. We read them at night when we go to bed. Our favorite character is Oki because he is a very good friend to Kendra and because he is an apprentice to Ratchet.

~ Max and Gus, 7 and 4

I loved your books! I finished the *Kendra* books in three days, they where so good! My favorite character is Uncle Griffinskitch because he stands his ground even when he is accused by Brownie (Burdock Brown) in the third book.

~ Turner, age 12

I love Kendra! This book is so magical! But I wish to know how old is Uncle Griffinskitch. I can't wait to see if the *Kendra* books continue!

~ Michelle, age 8

I am a big fan of yours and I adore all of your books. Your imagination is very inspiring and I love how you create creatures and the names and your story lines are breath-taking. Mr. Fodi, you are an amazing illustrator and writer.

~ Bakhtaawar, age 10

I just love your books. Can you make thousands of them? No, a million. No, a billion. No, a zillion! That would be great.

~ Amy, age 9

I really liked this book. I thought it was awesome, especially how the characters are always coming up with ideas to overcome obstacles. My favorite character is Trooogul because he acts so tough and argues with Kendra, but the arguing seems more like they're close friends than enemies. I didn't like how you left me hanging. I wouldn't have minded a longer book! I also wish you hadn't allowed Burdock Brown to be leader of the elders! However, overall I'd say these books are awesome! I hope Kendra's adventures never end!

~ Emma, age 11

Dear Mr. Wiz, I'm really looking forward to reading the fifth book. And my favorite character is Gayla because she is so adventurous. And I like Jinx because she makes funny names for Professor Bumblebean.

~ Melody, age 8

I love all your books in *The Chronicles of Kendra Kandlestar*. My favorite characters are Oki and Jinx. I like Oki because he is so cute and I like how he always thinks of vegetables! I like Jinx because she is fierce, not afraid and I like the funny names she calls Professor Bumblebean!

~ Andrea, age 9

Dear Mr. Fodi,
I LOVE your books! My favorite book is the Crack in Kazah. I really liked it when you kept Prince's name a secret. Before I got the Crack in the Kazah, I was wondering, What's Prince's name? I was really happy when I found out what prince's name was. My favorite bits are when Kendra goes to the future and when she meets Leemus Longshanks and when she tells uncle Griffinskitch to help her in the Rumble Pit and when she goes to the Rumble Pit and when she meets Gayla. And again I LOVE YOUR BOOKS!

~ Evie, age 7

I love the Kendra Kandlestar series. My favorite character is Oki because he's really funny.

~ Kaitlyn, age 8

I have finished *Crack in Kazah* and it was wonderful! I really want to rad your next book.

~ Grace, age 10

I just finished the third *Kendra Kandlestar* book and it was great! I just have a few questions to ask you. First of all, how is your fourth book of *Kendra Kandlestar* going? After I read the third one, I couldn't bear to wait for the next one. Secondly, have any monsters except for Prince Peryton and Trooogul been good, or will be good in your next few books. I really wanted a Krake or something a bit like it, but isn't as fat to be maybe used as a horse for Eens and is the suitable size for them. Lastly, is your fourth book cover going to be purple?
~ Matthew, age 10

Kendra Kandlestar books are one of my favorite books in the world. I feel very good contacting you and telling you what I think of your super duper, triple diple, fantastically awesome books.
~ Martina, age 9

I really love your work. I'm very excited to read the next book in the series. I was on the edge of my seat. The second one started where the last one last left off and I really liked that,it was very neat, from the escape of Pugglemud's mines I knew Trooogul was Kiro. The door was more like the plant that almost turned Oki into a onion. Later on I went back and figured out what creature everyone was. The third one was a rumbling tumbling spell for a disaster with Krakes. I think you saved the best for last in The Crack in Kazah.
~ Emma, age 9

I am a huge fan I love your books! My favorite character is Kendra because she is brave and goes to adventures.
~ Melynda, age 10

I read the 1st, 2nd and the 4th book. Your books are so good. I hope you write a 5th and 6th book. I like the 4th book the best. I like Kendra the best because she is not a normal Een. I also like Jinx and Oki and Uncle Griffinskitch. I like it when Kendra,Oki and Gayla are in the ocean. I am going to be Kendra for Halloween.

~ Marika, age 10

I have read two of your books your book are AMAZING! My favourite person is Oki he is cute and funny. Uncle Griffinskitch is funny too. Are you ever going to make a movie? And are you going to make another book?

~ Sedona, age 8

I like the books you wrote and illustrated. I really enjoyed them. I can't wait for Book 5. I had already read all the books. I wish you can write more books.

~ Hannah, age 7

I just finished reading your fourth book, *Kendra Kandlestar and the Crack in Kazah*. It was so good I just tried to finish it as fast as I could so I could read it again! My favourite characters are Oki and Kendra because they are best friends and they always have each other's back. Are you writing another book?

~Jasmin, age 11

I love *Kendra Kandlestar* books. You should write down six more series or more because they are amazing. So I was wondering if you could make *Kendra Kandlestar* movies! Please! Kendra Kandlestar is amazing and you are an amazing author.

~ Valeryia, age 9

Your books are so AWESOME! All of them: *Crack in Kazah, Door to Unger, Box of Whispers* and *Shard from Greeve*. My favorite characters are Kendra, Oki, Rachet, Uncle Griffin-skitch and Kayla. I like all of your stories and all of the parts in them! I think you are the BEST and that you are AWE-SOME! Your best fan and reader,

~ Alaya, age 9

Want to send your own Een-mail to Lee Edward Födi?
eenmail@kendrakandlestar.com

Or visit:
www.kendrakandlestar.com

Lee Edward Födi has been writing and illustrating stories about magic, monsters, and mystery for as long as he can remember. Growing up on a farm, he had many horrible chores, such as feeding chickens, collecting eggs, and cleaning the henhouse—all of which meant an epic battle each and every day with the farmyard rooster. Thankfully, the young author was one day able to fly the coop altogether. When he is not chronicling the land between here and there, "Mr. Wiz" (as he is so often called) spends his time speaking at schools and helping kids sculpt their own stories through writing workshops. He lives in Vancouver, Canada, and enjoys traveling to distant and exotic lands, where he can feel like he has slipped through the cracks of time and into the days of ancient history.

Find out more at www.leefodi.com and www.kendrakandlestar.com.